GERMAN
SHORT STORIES
IN THE BLACK FOREST
VOCABULARY PERFECTION SERIES

MASTER THE A1 VOCABULARY IN JUST 21 DAYS

BLACK SWAN LANGUAGES

Contents

Introduction

The Aims of This Book

"Übung macht den Meister."

The German proverb above translates directly into the English as, "Practice makes the master." In other words, the more meaningful effort one invests into learning a skill or craft, the better one will understand it.

We've created this book with the aim of delighting learners in search of real German short stories for a more self-directed learning approach, as well as those with the more singular focus of mastering the complete A1 level vocabulary.

A Suggested 21-Day Schedule

Days 1 thru 16: For the first sixteen days, a fast-track schedule could comprise of reading one short story chapter each day. It would also be prudent to utilize the featured vocabulary lists to learn as many words and phrases as possible while reading the stories. This will help to save you some time when you are finished with the stories and ready to tackle the full glossary.

Days 17 thru 21: In the final five days, a natural continuation of the fast-track schedule would focus on internalizing all of the vocabulary in the glossary following the short stories. Essentially, this glossary contains 650+ A1 level vocabulary based on the official list published by the Goethe Institute. (See the Resources chapter for a link to this publicly available online resource.) A balanced workload distribution would suggest that each of the five days should include internalizing at least 130 entries from the glossary. While many of the words will be familiar to those with previous German language study experience, it is also very doable for absolute beginners provided that ample time is set aside.

Important Disclaimers to Note

In the interest of an easier learning experience, several omissions have been purposefully made within our glossary. They are as follows:

- **Only the masculine forms of dual-gender nouns are listed.** Such nouns mostly refer to professions or specific roles which people carry out in their everyday lives. For a more advanced learning experience, feminine forms of German dual-gender nouns can be easily found online via a search using terms like "feminine of der Kellner," where the final two words are respectively the gender-specific definite article and the capitalized German noun.

- **The plural forms and parts of speech are also largely omitted.** However, one can deduce the part of speech to a great extent by the parenthetical elements associated with each vocabulary word. Vocabulary which include (der), (die), or (das) are always nouns, those which include (to) are always verbs, and those without parenthetical elements are adjectives, adverbs, prepositions, or something other than a noun or verb. Online German-English dictionaries are an invaluable resource to determine the oftentimes multiple parts of speech a particular word can encompass. Likewise, plural forms of German nouns can be easily found online via a search using terms like "plural of die Blume," where the final two words are respectively the gender-specific definite article and the capitalized German noun.

Don't agonize too much about the details of dual-gender nouns, plural forms, or parts of speech if this is your first time learning

German vocabulary. Just remember to relax, focus, and enjoy the rewarding process of your language acquisition journey!

Get Ready to Experience the Black Forest of Germany!

The subsequent chapters will feature a fun primer to the Black Forest region of Germany, an original map pinpointing the story locations, the sixteen short stories, and the complete A1 vocabulary glossary. Ready to improve your German language skills? Auf geht's! (Let's go!)

Welcome to the Black Forest...

Where in Germany Is the Black Forest?

The Black Forest (or, "Schwarzwald" in the German language) is a largely mountainous and tree-filled expanse of nature located completely within the southwesternmost German state of Baden-Württemberg. The Black Forest essentially shares its western border with eastern parts of France including the city of Strasbourg (where the European Parliament holds their meetings) and its southern border with northern parts of Switzerland including Basel (the birthplace of Roger Federer).

What Attractions Are in the Black Forest?

The Black Forest is home to countless attractions including historical castles such as the Hohenbaden Castle (constructed in the year 1102), exquisite museums like the Fabergé Museum (housing over 700 of the priceless eggs created by the famous

Russian jeweler Carl Fabergé), and perhaps most notably, the incredible variety of outdoor activities possible like hiking, boating, and skiing, and more!

Why Is This Region Called the Black Forest?

Believe it or not, according to a blog article published by the legendary Rick Steves, the Black Forest region had acquired its name from the ancient Romans. Because the forestry which had existed in this same space during their time was dense, dark, and mysterious, the ancient Romans reportedly called it "black." The name lives on today and attracts millions of visitors each year to the magical and invigorating oasis of natural splendors.

France

Germany

o KARLSRUHE

o STRASBOURG

Rhine

Faberge Museum

Westweg Trail

START

Mercedes-Benz Museum

Gertelbach Waterfalls

European Parliament

Hornisgrinde

World's Biggest Cuckoo Clock

The Black Forest Region

Europa-Park

Black Forest Museum

Titisee

Kaiserstuhl Vineyards

Schauinsland

Feldberg

Rhine

Euro Airport
Basel-Mulhouse-Freiburg

Switzerland

o BASEL

Rhine

Chapter 1

"Feldberg Friends" // "Feldberg Freunde"

Photo of Feldberg hikers by Andreas Zerndl.

Featured Vocabulary

am Fuße des Berges: at the foot of the mountain, **auf dem Weg nach oben**: on the way up, **beide**: both, **das stimmt**: that is correct, **der höchste Berg**: the tallest mountain, **der Mond**: the moon, **der Parkplatz**: the parking lot, **die frische Bergluft**: the fresh mountain air, **die ganze Wanderung**: the entire hike, **die Sonne**: the sun, **die Tannenbäume**: the fir trees, **die vier**: the four of them, **dreizehn Jahre alt**: thirteen years old, **ein beliebtes Ausflugsziel**: a popular attraction, **ein paar Sandwiches**: some sandwiches, **ein wunderbares Restaurant**: a wonderful restaurant, **eine Seilbahn**: a cable car ropeway, **eine Stunde**: an hour, **genau**: exactly, **genießen den Nachmittag**: enjoy the afternoon, **herrlich**: splendid, **ihre Lieblingswanderschuhe**: her favorite hiking shoes, **im Urlaub**: on vacation, **in der Finanzbranche**: in the financial industry, **in der Nähe**: nearby, **meine Frau und mein Sohn**: my wife and my son, **müde**: tired, **nach einem langen Tag**: after a long day, **natürlich**: of course, **nicht allein**: not alone, **nicht weit von hier**: not far from here, **Ninas Telefonnummer**: Nina's phone number, **Schwarzwälder Schinken**: Black Forest ham, **seine Familie**: his family, **viel leichter**: much easier, **viel schneller**: much faster, **viel steiler als**: much steeper than, **vielleicht**: maybe, **zu Abend**

essen: to have dinner, **zum ersten Mal**: for the first time, **zum Fuß des Feldbergs**: to the foot of the Feldberg, **zumindest**: at least, **zustimmend**: in agreement

Short Story: "Feldberg Friends"

Nina ist im Urlaub! Sie will auf den Feldberg wandern. Der Feldberg ist der höchste Berg in der Region Schwarzwald in Deutschland. Er ist ein beliebtes Ausflugsziel bei vielen Wanderern.

Nina is on vacation! She wants to hike the Feldberg. The Feldberg is the tallest mountain in the Black Forest region of Germany. It is a popular attraction with many hikers.

Nina fährt alleine mit ihrem Auto zum Feldberg. Sie packte ein paar Sandwiches, Obst und viel Wasser ein. Sie trägt ihre Lieblingswanderschuhe. Und natürlich hat sie auch ihre Kamera dabei.

Nina drives her car alone to the Feldberg. She packed some sandwiches, fruit, and a lot of water. She is wearing her favorite hiking shoes. And, of course, she also has her camera with her.

Der Parkplatz ist mit vielen Autos gefüllt. Nina geht zu den anderen Wanderern am Fuße des Berges. Es gibt eine

Seilbahn, die auf den Gipfel führt. Nina möchte aber lieber die ganze Wanderung zu Fuß machen.

The parking lot is filled with many cars. Nina walks towards the other hikers at the foot of the mountain. There is a cable car ropeway that goes to the summit. However, Nina would rather do the entire hike by foot.

Auf dem Weg nach oben sieht Nina einen Mann, der sich ausstreckt. Er scheint die frische Bergluft zu genießen.

On the way up, Nina sees a man stretching out. He seems to be enjoying the fresh mountain air.

„Der Feldberg ist viel steiler als ich erwartet habe!", sagt er zu Nina. „Bist du auch zum ersten Mal hier?"

"The Feldberg is much steeper than I expected!", he says to Nina. "Are you here for the first time too?"

„Ja, das stimmt", antwortet Nina. „Es ist sicherlich eine anspruchsvolle Wanderung!"

"Yes, that is correct," replies Nina. "It's certainly a challenging hike!"

„Genau! Zumindest für das nächste Mal weiß ich es besser", sagt der Mann.

"Exactly! I know better for the next time, at least," says the man.

„Bist du allein gekommen?", fragt Nina.

"Did you come by yourself?", asks Nina.

Der Mann schüttelt den Kopf. Er zeigt weiter oben auf den Weg. „Meine Frau und mein Sohn sind viel schneller als ich", lacht er.

The man shakes his head. He points further up the path. "My wife and my son are much faster than me," he laughs.

„Wie heißen Sie?", fragt Nina den Mann. „Mein Name ist Nina. Ich freue mich, Sie kennenzulernen."

"What is your name?", Nina asks the man. "My name is Nina. I'm pleased to meet you."

Der Mann streckt seine Hand aus. „Und ich heiße Johann. Ich freue mich auch, Sie kennenzulernen!"

The man stretches out his hand. "And my name is Johann. I'm pleased to meet you too!"

Sie schütteln sich die Hände.

They shake hands.

Nina und Johann wandern weiter den Feldberg hinauf. Bald

holen sie Johanns Familie ein. Johann stellt Nina dann seine Frau Monika und seinen Sohn Till vor. Monika fragt Nina, ob sie mit der Familie wandern möchte.

Nina and Johann hike further up the Feldberg. They soon catch up with Johann's family. Johann then introduces Nina to his wife, Monika, and his son, Till. Monika asks Nina if she would like to hike together with the family.

Die vier haben viel Spaß zusammen. Die Wanderung ist viel leichter, wenn man nicht allein ist. Nina schätzt sich glücklich, Johann und seine Familie kennengelernt zu haben.

The four of them have a lot of fun together. The hike is much easier when one is not alone. Nina feels fortunate to have met Johann and his family.

Johann, Monika und Till wohnen in Frankfurt am Main. Johann und Monika sind beide in ihren Vierzigern. Beide sind auch in der Finanzbranche tätig. Till ist dreizehn Jahre alt und geht gerne zur Schule.

Johann, Monika, and Till reside in Frankfurt on the Main. Johann and Monika are both in their forties. They also both work in the financial industry. Till is thirteen years old and enjoys going to school.

Eine Stunde vergeht, während sie weiterwandern. Und sie sind dem Gipfel schon sehr nahe!

An hour passes as they continue hiking. And they are already very close to the summit!

Die vier genießen den Nachmittag auf dem Gipfel. Sie lieben die spektakuläre Aussichten. Alle wollen wieder auf den Feldberg kommen. Die kühle, frische Brise ist herrlich!

The four of them enjoy the afternoon on the summit. They love the spectacular views. Everyone wants to come back to the Feldberg again. The chilly, fresh breeze is splendid!

Schließlich geht die Sonne langsam unter. Nina, Monika, Johann und Till gehen zurück zum Fuß des Feldbergs.

Eventually, the sun slowly sinks. Nina, Monika, Johann, and Till walk back down to the foot of the Feldberg.

„So ist es viel leichter!", sagt Johann. Alle lachen zustimmend.

"It's much easier this way!", says Johann. Everyone laughs in agreement.

Sie kommen wieder in der Nähe der Talstation der Feldbergbahn an.

They arrive back nearby the valley station of the Feldberg train.

„Vielleicht können wir zusammen zu Abend essen?", fragt Monika. „Nicht weit von hier gibt es ein wunderbares Restaurant."

"Maybe we can have dinner together?", asks Monika. "There is a wonderful restaurant not far from here."

Nina strahlt. „Das würde ich gerne!"

Nina beams. "I would love that!"

Das Restaurant serviert regionale Spezialitäten. Auf der Speisekarte stehen Schwarzwälder Schinken in Sauce, marinierter Fisch und sogar eine klassische Schwarzwälder Kirschtorte!

The restaurant serves regional specialties. The menu features Black Forest ham in sauce, marinated fish, and even a classic Black Forest cherry cake!

Nach einem herzhaften Abendessen ist es Zeit, sich zu verabschieden. Nina bedankt sich bei Johanns Familie für den schönen gemeinsamen Tag. Johann und Monika fragen nach Ninas Telefonnummer, damit sie in Kontakt bleiben können.

After enjoying a hearty dinner, it's time to say goodbye. Nina thanks Johann's family for the beautiful day together. Johann and Monika ask for Nina's phone number so that they can stay in touch.

Nina geht zurück zu ihrem Auto. Die Luft ist wohltuend und der Mond scheint durch die Tannenbäume. Nina ist nach einem langen Tag müde. Aber sie ist froh, heute auf den Feldberg gekommen zu sein!

Nina walks back to her car. The air is soothing and the moon is shining through the fir trees. Nina is tired after a long day. But she is happy to have come to the Feldberg today!

Chapter 2

"A Special Place" // "Ein Besonderer Ort"

Photo of the Mummelsee by Heinz-Peter Schwerin.

Featured Vocabulary

als auch: and, **besonderer Ort**: special place, **das Paar**: the couple, **das Zwitschern der Vögel**: the chirping of birds, **der Weg**: the trail, **die Autofahrt**: the car ride, **die Bäume**: the trees, **eigentlich**: actually, **ein älterer Mann**: an older man, **ein bisschen hungrig**: a bit hungry, **ein Ehepaar**: a married couple, **ein schöner See**: a beautiful lake, **eine Platte mit lokalem Käse**: a plate of local cheese, **eine Weile**: a while, **einfach**: absolutely, **Einheimische**: locals, **gute Idee**: good idea, **hinter den Wolken**: behind the clouds, **ihre Hunde**: your dogs, **ihren Enkeln**: their grandchildren, **ihren Hochzeitstag**: their wedding anniversary, **Kartoffelcremesoupe**: potato cream soup, **lokalen Spezialitäten**: local specialties, **mein Deutscher Schäferhund**: my German Shepherd, **meine Kindheitstage**: my childhood days, **Pilzravioli**: mushroom ravioli, **sauber und frisch**: clean and fresh, **Schatz**: darling, **sehr gut trainiert**: very well-trained, **sehr intelligente Rassen**: very intelligent breeds, **sitzen an einem Tisch**: sit at a table, **sowohl**: both, **spektakulär**: spectacular, **Steak mit Preiselbeeren**: steak with cranberries, **unser besonderer Ort**: our special place, **über eine Stunde**: over an hour, **vor vierzig Jahren**: forty years ago, **wiederkommen**: come back again

Short Story: "A Special Place"

Heinrich und Gisela sind ein Ehepaar. Sie trafen sich auf der Hornisgrinde im Schwarzwald. Das war vor vierzig Jahren. Heute werden sie dort ihren Hochzeitstag feiern.

Heinrich and Gisela are a married couple. They met at the Hornisgrinde in the Black Forest. It was forty years ago. Today, they will celebrate their wedding anniversary there.

Das Paar genießt die Autofahrt zur Hornisgrinde. Die Luft is sauber und frisch. Die Bäume sind grün. Es sind sowohl Touristen als auch Einheimische unterwegs.

The couple enjoys the car ride to the Hornisgrinde. The air is clean and fresh. The trees are verdant. There are both tourists and locals out and about.

Die Fahrt dauert über eine Stunde. Schließlich kommen sie an ihrem besonderen Ort an. Sie beginnen schnell zu laufen. Der Weg ist eigentlich eine Schleife.

The drive takes over an hour. They finally arrive at their special place. They quickly start walking. The trail is actually a loop.

Romantik liegt in der Luft. „Die Ansichten vom Gipfel wird

spektakulär sein", sagt Gisela.

Romance is in the air. "The views from the summit will be spectacular," says Gisela.

„Ich weiß, dass sie es sein werden!", lächelt Heinrich. „Erinnern Sie sich daran, dass es bewölkt war, als wir uns trafen?"

"I know they will be!", smiles Heinrich. "Do you remember how it was overcast when we met?"

„Ja, natürlich erinnere ich mich daran", antwortet Gisela. „Aber die Sonne kam schließlich hinter den Wolken hervor, nicht wahr?"

"Yes, of course I remember that," replies Gisela. "But the sun eventually came out from behind the clouds, didn't it?"

Heinrich und Gisela lachen eine Weile zusammen. Das Zwitschern der Vögel erfüllt die Luft.

Heinrich and Gisela laugh together for a while. The chirping of birds fill the air.

Ein älterer Mann geht neben Heinrich und Gisela mit seinen beiden großen Hunden spazieren. „Ihre Hunde sind sehr gut trainiert", sagt Gisela zu ihm.

An older man alongside Heinrich and Gisela is walking his two large dogs. "Your dogs are very well-trained," Gisela tells him.

„Schön, Sie kennenzulernen", sagt der Mann. „August ist mein Dobermann und Hugo ist mein Deutscher Schäferhund. Beides sind sehr intelligente Rassen."

"Nice to meet you", says the man. "August is my Doberman and Hugo is my German Shepherd. Both are very intelligent breeds."

August und Hugo beschnüffeln beide das Paar. Heinrich lässt sie seine Hand ablecken.

August and Hugo both sniff the couple. Heinrich lets them lick his hand.

Gisela sagt: „Schatz, lass uns runter zum Mummelsee gehen! Ich bin ein bisschen hungrig".

Gisela says, "Darling, let's go down to the Mummelsee! I'm a bit hungry."

„Das ist eine gute Idee", antwortet Heinrich. „Die lokalen Spezialitäten im Hotelrestaurant schmecken einfach köstlich!"

"That's a good idea," replies Heinrich. "The local specialties at the hotel restaurant are absolutely delightful!"

Die beiden sitzen an einem Tisch im Hotelrestaurant. Gisela bestellt Pilzravioli und eine Platte mit lokalem Käse. Heinrich bestellt eine Kartoffelcremesoupe und ein Steak mit Preiselbeeren.

The two sit at a table inside the hotel restaurant. Gisela orders mushroom ravioli and a plate of local cheese. Heinrich orders a potato cream soup and a steak with cranberries.

„Der Mummelsee ist so ein schöner See", sagt Gisela zu Heinrich. „Er erinnert mich an meine Kindheitstage."

"The Mummelsee is such a beautiful lake," Gisela tells Heinrich. "It reminds me of my childhood days."

Heinrich antwortet: „Ich bin froh, Sie hier vor so langer Zeit kennengelernt zu haben. Ich möchte wiederkommen. Es ist unser besonderer Ort."

Heinrich replies, "I'm happy to have met you here so long ago. I want to come back again. It's our special place."

Die beiden unterhalten sich noch eine Weile. Dann ist es Zeit, nach Hause zu gehen und ihren Enkeln von ihrem besonderen Tag zu erzählen.

The two of them talk for a while longer. Then, it's time to return home and tell their grandchildren about their special day.

Chapter 3

"Winter Wonderland" // "Winterwunderland"

Photo of snowy Feldberg by Johannes Erb.

Featured Vocabulary

am frühen Nachmittag: by the early afternoon, **automatisch**: automatically, **bald wiederkommen**: come back again soon, **danach**: after that, **dann**: then, **das Abenteuer**: the adventure, **das warme Essen**: the warm food, **deine Füße**: your feet, **die Kinder**: the children, **die leeren Sitze**: the empty seats, **die Rechnung**: the bill, **ein eiskalter Wind**: an icy cold wind, **ein paar Minuten später**: a few minutes later, **fühlt sich unsicher**: feels unsteady, **glücklich**: happy, **im Auto**: in the car, **in bar**: in cash, **in der Nähe**: closeby, **irgendwo auf den Weg**: somewhere along the way, **kleine Ort**: small town, **mit einem Lächeln**: with a smile, **morgen**: tomorrow, **müde und hungrig**: tired and hungry, **nicht alleine**: not alone, **nicht verletzt**: not injured, **noch Anfänger**: still beginners, **noch skeptisch**: still skeptical, **plötzlich**: suddenly, **Pommes frites**: French fries, **seine Mutter**: his mother, **Skifahren gehen**: go skiing, **so viel Spaß**: so much fun, **spielen**: play, **Suppe und einen Burger**: soup and a burger, **viel los**: a lot going on, **viele andere Kinder**: many other children, **viele Leute**: many people, **von einem lustigen Skitag**: about a fun day of skiing, **vor allem**: especially, **wie ein Stück Pizza**: like a slice of pizza, **wirklich**: really, **wo**: where, **wohnt in Todtnau**: lives in Todtnau, **zusammen**: together

Short Story: "Winter Wonderland"

Familie Neumann wohnt in Todtnau. Sie lieben den Schnee, vor allem die Kinder Emily und Max. Sie spielen stundenlang im Schnee herum. Der kleine Ort Todtnau ist nicht weit vom Feldberg entfernt, wo man im Winter besonders gut Skifahren kann.

The Neumann family lives in Todtnau. They love the snow, especially the children, Emily and Max. They play around in the snow for hours. The small town of Todtnau isn't far from Feldberg, where one can ski particularly well in winter.

Vater Timo und Mutter Sybille haben dieses Jahr einen Plan: sie wollen mit Emily und Max Skifahren gehen. Die Kinder können das noch nicht, aber das lernen sie bestimmt schnell.

Father Timo and Mother Sybille have a plan this year: they want to go skiing with Emily and Max. The children can't do it yet, but they will surely learn it quickly.

Heute fahren die vier zum Feldberg. Doch sie sind nicht alleine. Überall sind Menschen, die Spaß haben. Es ist definitiv viel los.

Today, the four of them are heading to the Feldberg. But they are not alone. There are people everywhere having fun. There's definitely a lot going on.

„Es sind viele Leute hier!", sagt Max.

"There are a lot of people here!", says Max.

Timo nickt. „Nicht nur wir wollen Skifahren. Viele andere Kinder lernen es auch."

Timo nods. "Not only we want to ski. Many other children are also learning it."

Emily und Max finden das toll.

Emily and Max think that's great.

Zuerst leihen sie sich die Ausrüstung zum Skifahren aus. Es ist nicht einfach, die Stiefel anzuziehen. Sybille kippt sogar einmal fast um. Aber danach sind alle bereit!

First, they borrow the equipment for skiing. It's not easy to get the boots on. Sybille even almost falls over once. But after that, everyone is ready!

Sie freuen sich sehr. Jetzt beginnt das Abenteuer wirklich! Zuerst müssen sie mit dem Lift auf den Gipfel fahren. Aber Emily hat plötzlich keine Lust mehr.

They are very happy. Now the adventure really begins! First they have to take the lift to the summit. But Emily suddenly doesn't feel like it anymore.

„Weißt du nicht, was du machen sollst?", fragt Timo sie.

"Do you not know what you should do?", Timo asks her.

Emily schüttelt den Kopf. „Nein, weiß ich nicht."

Emily shakes her head. "No, I don't know."

Timo nimmt sie an die Hand. „Also, von oben kommen die leeren Sitze herunter. Wir stellen uns einfach davor und setzen uns hin. Dann schließen wir den Bügel und fahren automatisch den Berg hinauf."

Timo takes her by the hand. "So, the empty seats come down from the top. We simply stand in front of it and sit down. Then we close the bar and automatically ride up the mountain."

Emily ist noch skeptisch, aber sie kommt mit.

Emily is still skeptical, but she comes along.

Ein paar Minuten später steht Familie Neumann oben auf dem Gipfel. Ein eiskalter Wind weht um ihre Nasen. Max fühlt sich unsicher auf seinen Skiern. Sybille hält ihn fest.

A few minutes later, the Neumann family is standing at the top of the summit. An icy cold wind blows around their noses. Max feels unsteady on his skis. Sybille holds him tight.

„Und jetzt fahren wir den Berg hinunter", sagt seine Mutter zu ihm.

"And now we're going down the mountain," his mother says to him.

„Wie halte ich an?", fragt Emily.

"How do I stop?", asks Emily.

Timo zeigt es ihr. „Du musst deine Füße wie ein Stück Pizza machen." Er zeigt es seinen Kindern. Max und Emily lachen vor Freude.

Timo shows her. "You have to make your feet like a slice of pizza." He shows his children. Max and Emily laugh with delight.

Die Eltern leiten ihre Kinder an. Die Familie Neumann geht gemeinsam den Berg hinunter. Irgendwo auf den Weg fällt Max hin. Glücklicherweise ist er nicht verletzt!

The parents both guide their children. The Neumann family goes down the mountain together. Max falls down somewhere along the way. Luckily, he is not injured!

Dann geht der Spaß weiter. Emily und Max sind beide noch Anfänger. Aber sie lieben den Schnee wirklich!

Then, the fun continues on. Emily and Max are both still beginners. But they really love the snow!

Am frühen Nachmittag sind alle müde und hungrig. Sie gehen zu einem Restaurant in der Nähe. Die Kinder essen beide Pommes frites. Die Eltern essen beide Suppe und einen Burger. Alle sind dankbar für das warme Essen.

By the early afternoon, everyone is tired and hungry. They walk to a restaurant closeby. The kids both eat French fries. The parents both eat soup and a burger. Everyone is grateful for the warm food.

Max möchte wieder Skifahren gehen. „Können wir bald wiederkommen?", fragt er laut.

Max wants to go skiing again. "Can we come back again soon?", he asks aloud.

„Ja, natürlich können wir das", antwortet Sybille mit einem Lächeln.

"Yes, of course we can," replies Sybille with a smile.

Sie bezahlen die Rechnung in bar. Dann fährt die Familie

Neumann wieder nach Hause. Die Kinder sind im Auto schnell eingeschlafen. Die beiden träumen von einem lustigen Skitag am Feldberg.

They pay the bill in cash. Then the Neumann family drives back home. The kids quickly fall asleep in the car. They both dream about a fun day of skiing at the Feldberg.

Chapter 4

"The Waterfalls" // "Die Wasserfälle"

Photo of Gertelbach Waterfalls by Frank Fischbach.

Featured Vocabulary

am Bahnhof Baden-Baden: at the Baden-Baden train station, **an seine Oma**: to his grandma, **auf eine Bank**: on a bench, **danke**: thanks, **das Porto**: the postage, **das Rauschen der Wasserfälle**: the sound of the waterfalls, **die Fahrt**: the ride, **dorthin**: to there, **ein alter Mann**: an old man, **ein Junge**: a boy, **eine Fahrkarte**: a ride ticket, **endlich fertig**: finally finished, **erholt sich**: recovers, **es tut mir leid**: I'm sorry, **etwa eine Stunde**: about an hour, **fasziniert von**: fascinated by, **Freundlichkeit**: kindness, **Ihre Großmutter**: your grandmother, **im Krankenhaus**: in the hospital, **kann nicht viel tun**: can't do much, **kaum jemand**: hardly anyone, **lächelnd**: with a smile, **leichter**: easier, **mein Name ist**: my name is, **mit der S-Bahn**: by suburban rail, **nähert sich**: approaches, **schön und friedlich**: nice and peaceful, **seine Frau**: his wife, **setzt sich neben**: sits down next to, **tiefe Gedanken**: deep thoughts, **vielen Dank**: thank you so much, **viel Glück**: good luck, **viel Spaß**: have fun, **wie aus dem Nichts**: from seemingly nowhere, **wie heißen Sie**: what is your name, **zum Abendessen**: for dinner, **zum Postamt am Bahnhof**: to the post office at the train station, **zwanzig Minuten**: twenty minutes, **zwei Wochen**: two weeks

Short Story: "The Waterfalls"

Peter besucht heute die Gertelbach-Wasserfälle. Am Bahnhof Baden-Baden kauft er eine Fahrkarte. Er fährt mit der S-Bahn dorthin.

Peter is visiting the Gertelbach Waterfalls today. He buys a ride ticket at the Baden-Baden train station. He is traveling to there by suburban rail.

Die Fahrt dauert etwa eine Stunde. Er steigt in Bühl in den Bus um. Von der Bushaltestelle Bühlertal läuft er etwa zwanzig Minuten zu den Wasserfällen.

The ride takes about an hour. He transfers to the bus in Bühl. From the Bühlertal bus stop, he walks about twenty minutes to the waterfalls.

Bald hört er das Rauschen der Wasserfälle. Peter gefällt es hier. Das Ambiente ist schön und friedlich.

Soon, he hears the sound of the waterfalls. Peter loves it here. The ambience is nice and peaceful.

Es ist heute kaum jemand hier. Das macht es leichter, tiefe Gedanken zu haben.

There is hardly anyone here today. This makes it easier to have deep thoughts.

Peter möchte einen Brief an seine Oma schreiben. Sie ist schon seit zwei Wochen krank. Er möchte ihr helfen, sich besser zu fühlen.

Peter wants to write a letter to his grandma. She has been ill for two weeks. He wants to help her feel better.

Peter setzt sich auf eine Bank. Er überlegt, was er schreiben soll. Wie aus dem Nichts kommen ein alter Mann und ein Junge zu Peter.

Peter sits down on a bench. He is thinking of what he should write. From seemingly nowhere, an old man and a boy come to Peter.

„Wie geht es Ihnen?", fragt der alte Mann.

"How are you doing?", asks the old man.

„Es könnte besser sein. Und Sie?", antwortet Peter lächelnd.

"Things could be better. And you?", replies Peter with a smile.

Der alte Mann setzt sich neben Peter auf die Bank. Der Junge ist fasziniert von den Wasserfällen.

The old man sits down next to Peter on the bench. The boy is fascinated by the waterfalls.

Peter sagt dem alten Mann: „Ich schreibe einen Brief für meine Oma. Wir sind hier zusammen gewandert. Jetzt liegt sie im Krankenhaus und kann nicht viel tun."

Peter tells the old man, "I'm writing a letter for my grandma. We've hiked here together. Now, she's in the hospital and can't do much."

„Es tut mir leid, das über Ihre Großmutter zu hören. Ich hoffe, sie erholt sich bald!", sagt der alte Mann.

"I'm sorry to hear that about your grandmother. I hope she recovers soon!", says the old man.

„Vielen Dank für Ihre Freundlichkeit", sagt Peter. „Das hoffe ich auch sehr! Darf ich fragen, wie Sie heißen?"

"Thank you so much for your kindness", replies Peter. "I really hope so too! May I ask what your name is?"

„Mein Name ist Günter. Und wie heißen Sie?"

"My name is Günter. And what is your name?"

„Peter. Es ist schön, Sie kennenzulernen."

"Peter. It's wonderful to meet you."

Der Junge nähert sich seinem Großvater. Günter sagt zu Peter: „Okay, wir müssen noch wandern gehen. Viel Glück mit Ihrem Brief!"

The boy approaches his grandfather. Gunter tells Peter, "Okay, we still need to go hiking. Good luck with your letter!"

Peter lächelt und winkt. „Danke, und viel Spaß beim Wandern!"

Peter smiles and waves, "Thanks, and have fun hiking!"

Peter genießt die Wasserfälle und schreibt den Brief an seine Oma. Und der Brief ist endlich fertig!

Peter enjoys the waterfalls and writes the letter to his grandma. And the letter is finally finished!

Er bringt den Brief zum Postamt am Bahnhof. Er bezahlt das Porto und der Brief ist auf dem Weg!

He takes the letter to the post office at the train station. He pays for the postage and the letter is on its way!

Er denkt daran, die Wasserfälle wieder mit seiner Oma zu besuchen. Dann fragt er sich, was seine Frau zum Abendessen kocht!

He thinks about visiting the waterfalls again with his grandma.

Then, he wonders what his wife is cooking for dinner!

Chapter 5

"Wedding at the Titisee" //
"Hochzeit am Titisee"

Photo of the Titisee by Amnach Kinchokawat.

Featured Vocabulary

als Geschenk mitbringen: bring along as a gift, **am Ufer des Titisee**: at the shore of the Titisee, **der Bräutigam**: the groom, **der große Tag**: the big day, **die Einladung**: the invitation, **die Familie Reiter**: the Reiter family, **die Reiters übernachten**: the Reiters are staying overnight, **die vier**: the four of them, **einem beliebten See**: a popular lake, **ein toller Tag**: a great day, **eine richtige Party**: a real party, **es wäre toll**: it would be great, **Familie Reiterfast jeder**: almost everyone, **fern oder einen Film**: TV or a movie, **für zwei Nächte**: for two nights, **geht ins Bad**: goes into the bathroom, **Geld**: money, **glitzert im Mondlicht**: glistens in the moonlight, **herzlich willkommen**: hearty welcome, **ich weiß nicht**: I don't know, **Kuchen und Getränken**: cake and drinks, **lange aufbleiben**: stay up late, **mit einem breiten Lächeln**: with a big smile, **mit Oma und Opa**: with Grandma and Grandpa, **seine Nummer**: his number, **so lecker**: so delicious, **über die Hochzeit**: about the wedding, **um 15:00 Uhr**: at 3 p.m., **vielen Dank**: thank you very much, **wir gehen raus**: we're going outside, **zur Rezeption**: to the reception desk, **zurück im Hotel**: back at the hotel

Short Story: "Wedding at the Titisee"

Die Familie Reiter ist zu einer Hochzeit eingeladen. Deswegen fahren sie extra nach Neustadt. Die Stadt liegt direkt am Titisee, einem beliebten See im Schwarzwald.

The Reiter family has been invited to a wedding. That's why they are making a special trip to Neustadt. The town is located directly at the Titisee, a popular lake in the Black Forest.

Die Reiters übernachten über das Wochenende in einem Hotel. Sie kommen mit dem Auto an und gehen zur Rezeption.

The Reiters are staying overnight at a hotel for the weekend. They arrive by car and go to the reception desk.

„Herzlich willkommen!", sagt der Hotelier. „Haben Sie reserviert?"

"Hearty welcome!", says the hotelier. "Do you have a reservation?"

Papa Ulrich nickt. „Ja, auf den Namen Reiter."

Dad Ulrich nods. "Yes, in the name of Reiter."

Der Hotelier schaut auf seinem Computer nach. „Ah, ja. Wie ist Ihr Vorname?"

The hotelier checks his computer. "Ah, yes. What is your first name?"

„Ulrich.“

"Ulrich."

„Genau. Sie haben für zwei Nächte reserviert. Ich kann Ihnen anbieten, dass wir Ihr Gepäck direkt auf das Zimmer bringen. Sollen wir das tun?“

"Exactly. You have a reservation for two nights. I can offer to take your luggage directly to your room. Shall we do this?"

Die Kinder, Tina und Paul, rufen laut „Ja!“. Sie wollen nichts tragen.

The children, Tina and Paul, loudly shout "Yes!". They don't want to carry anything.

Der Hotelier lacht. „Wir freuen uns, Sie als unsere Gäste begrüßen zu dürfen!“

The hotelier laughs. "We look forward to welcoming you as our guests!"

„Vielen Dank!“, sagen Papa Ulrich und Mama Martina. Sie bekommen den Schlüssel.

"Thank you very much!", say Dad Ulrich and Mom Martina. They receive the key.

In ihrem Zimmer packt Familie Reiter alles aus.

The Reiter family unpacks everything in their room.

Paul legt sich in sein Bett. „Ich gehe nicht mehr raus. Ich schaue nur fern oder einen Film."

Paul lies down in his bed. "I'm not going out anymore. I'm just going to watch TV or a movie."

„Nein, wir gehen raus und schauen uns den Titisee an", sagt Martina und lächelt.

"No, we're going outside to look at the Titisee," Martina says and smiles.

„Ich muss auf die Toilette!", sagt Tina und geht ins Bad.

"I have to go to the toilet!", says Tina and goes into the bathroom.

„Danach gehen wir!", sagt Ulrich ungeduldig.

"After that, we're going!", says Ulrich impatiently.

Das Wetter ist perfekt! Es ist warm und die Sonne scheint. Die Reiters laufen lange durch Neustadt. Am Ufer des Titisee setzen sie sich in ein Café. Sie bestellen Kuchen und Martina

trinkt ein Bier dazu.

The weather is perfect! It's warm and the sun is shining. The Reiters walk for a long time through Neustadt. The sit down in a café at the shore of the Titisee. They order cake and Martina drinks a beer with it.

Paul zeigt auf das Wasser. „Kann ich da schwimmen gehen?"

Paul points to the water. "Can I go swimming there?"

„Ich weiß nicht", antwortet Ulrich. „Das ist vielleicht verboten."

"I don't know," replies Ulrich. "That might be forbidden."

„Es wäre toll", sagt Paul. Er schwimmt gern.

"It would be great," says Paul. He loves swimming.

Der Kuchen war so lecker. Martina bezahlt mit ihrer Debitkarte. Die vier gehen dann am See spazieren.

The cake was so delicious. Martina pays with her debit card. The four of them then go for a walk by the lake.

„Ich will mit Oma und Opa hier Urlaub machen. Dieser See ist so schön!", sagt Tina mit einem breiten Lächeln. „Man kann sogar den Feldberg sehen!"

"I want to vacation here with Grandma and Grandpa. This lake is so beautiful!", Tina says with a big smile. "One can even see the Feldberg!"

Zurück im Hotel, spricht die Familie Reiter über die Hochzeit. Morgen ist der große Tag. Alle sind aufgeregt.

Back at the hotel, the Reiter family talks about the wedding. Tomorrow is the big day. Everyone is excited.

„Wo ist die Einladung? Wann geht es los?", fragt Martina.

"Where is the invitation? When does it start?", asks Martina.

Ulrich sucht nach der Einlandung. „Um 15:00 Uhr", antwortet er.

Ulrich looks for the invitation. "At 3 p.m.", he replies.

Tina freut sich darauf. „Ich will viel tanzen!"

Tina is looking forward to it. "I want to dance a lot!"

„Was können wir als Geschenk mitbringen?", fragt Paul.

"What can we bring along as a gift?", asks Paul.

„Wir schenken Geld. Das macht fast jeder", sagt Martina.

"We give money as a gift. Almost everyone does that," says

Martina.

Ulrich steht von seinem Bett auf. „Ich möchte Klaus anrufen und fragen, wie es ihm geht." Klaus ist der Bräutigam. Ulrich wählt seine Nummer. Die Leitung ist besetzt. Ulrich versucht es später wieder.

Ulrich gets up from his bed. "I want to call Klaus and ask how he's doing." Klaus is the groom. Ulrich dials his number. The line is busy. Ulrich tries again later.

Am Abend isst die Familie Reiter im Hotelrestaurant. Der Titisee glitzert im Mondlicht.

In the evening, the Reiter family dines in the hotel restaurant. The Titisee glistens in the moonlight.

„Dürfen wir morgen lange aufbleiben?", fragt Paul beim Abendessen.

"May we stay up late tomorrow?", Paul asks over dinner.

„Klar!", sagt Ulrich. „Das wird eine richtige Party!"

"Sure!", says Ulrich. "It's going to be a real party!"

Am nächsten Morgen frühstücken sie gemeinsam. Und dann verkleiden sie sich. Sie wollen am besten aussehen. Eine

Hochzeit am Titisee — es wird ein toller Tag!

The next morning, they eat breakfast together. And then they get dressed up. They want to look their best. A wedding at the Titisee — it's going to be a great day!

Chapter 6

"Fun at the Theme Park" // "Spaß im Freizeitpark"

Photo of Europa Park by Vladislav Gajic.

Featured Vocabulary

alle Achterbahnen: all rollercoasters, **am Eingang**: at the entrance, **an der Kasse**: at the cash register, **an einem Kiosk**: at a kiosk, **auf der ganzen Welt**: all around the world, **beide Eltern**: both parents, **das echte Europa**: the real Europe, **der Dame**: to the lady, **ein kleiner Zug**: a small train, **Ein Mann**: a man, **ein paar Familienfotos**: some family photos, **eine gute Idee**: a good idea, **eine Karte**: a map, **Eis, Würstchen und Kartoffeln**: ice cream, sausages, and potatoes, **es ist bereits**: it's already, **fast eine Stunde**: almost an hour, **fast Sonnenuntergang**: almost sunset, **ihr Bruder**: her brother, **in den riesigen Park**: into the enormous park, **in der Schlange**: in the queue, **in einem anderen Land**: in another country, **Leas Vater**: Lea's father, **Lust auf Mittagessen**: desire for lunch, **müssen heute nicht arbeiten**: don't have to work today, **nicht erlaubt**: not allowed, **Orangensaft**: orange juice, **sie sind froh**: they're happy, **so viel Spaß**: so much fun, **so viel zu sehen**: so much to see, **Sommerferien**: summer vacation, **später**: later, **tolle Sachen**: great things, **viele verschiedene Länder**: many different countries, **wie Deutschland**: like Germany, **wie lange**: how long, **wollen wiederkommen**: want to come back again, **zu einer anderen Attraktion**: to another attraction

Short Story: "Fun at the Theme Park"

Heute ist ein besonderer Tag. Lea und ihr Bruder Finn gehen in den Europa-Park! Er ist auf der ganzen Welt bekannt. Ihre Eltern müssen heute nicht arbeiten und gehen mit.

Today is a special day. Lea and her brother, Finn, are going to Europa Park! It is well-known all around the world. Their parents don't have to work today and are going with them.

Bald stehen sie am Eingang. Leas Vater gibt der Dame an der Kasse das Geld. Sie dürfen in den riesigen Park.

They are soon standing at the entrance. Lea's father gives the money to the lady at the cash register. They are allowed into the enormous park.

„Wohin wollt ihr zuerst?", fragt Leas Mutter Nadine. Beide Eltern waren schon einmal im Europa-Park.

"Where do you want to go to first?", asks Lea's mother, Nadine. Both parents have been to Europa Park before.

Finn und Lea rufen: „Achterbahn fahren!" Aufgeregt laufen sie auf eine zu.

Finn and Lea shout: "Ride the rollercoaster!" They excitedly walk towards one.

Überall gibt es tolle Sachen. Lea spürt, dass etwas anders ist. „Mama, sind wir in einem anderen Land? Der Park sieht nicht wie Deutschland aus."

There are great things everywhere. Lea senses that something is different. "Mom, are we in another country? The park doesn't look like Germany."

Nadine lacht. „Der Europa-Park hat viele verschiedene Länder, wie das echte Europa!"

Nadine laughs. "Europa Park has many different countries, like the real Europe!"

„Wie interessant!", ruft Lea. Sie ist tief in Gedanken versunken.

"How interesting!", exclaims Lea. She is deep in thought.

Sie stehen in der Schlange vor der ersten Achterbahn. Sie haben fast eine Stunde gewartet.

They are standing in the queue at the first rollercoaster. They've been waiting almost an hour.

„Wie lange müssen wir stehen?" Finn will seine Beine

ausruhen. Es ist anstrengend.

"How long must we stand?" Finn wants to rest his legs. It is exhausting.

„Wir sind gleich dran", sagt Michael. Er kauft Getränke an einem Kiosk. Die Kinder trinken gerne Orangensaft.

"We're almost there," says Michael. He buys drinks at a kiosk. The children are happy to drink orange juice.

Endlich sind sie dran. Lea, Finn, Nadine und Michael sitzen zusammen im Wagen. Ein Mann macht die Bügel zu und drückt auf einen Schalter. Die Fahrt ist wild. Alle schreien vor Freude!

It's finally their turn. Lea, Finn, Nadine, and Michael sit together in the car. A man closes the bars and presses a switch. The ride is wild. Everyone screams in delight!

Dann fahren sie zu einer anderen Attraktion. Ein kleiner Zug bringt sie dorthin. Finn reibt sich die Augen. Er ist müde und will eine Pause machen. Das ist eine gute Idee! Es ist bereits 13 Uhr.

Then they go to another attraction. A small train takes them there. Finn rubs his eyes. He is tired and wants to take a break. That's a good idea! It's already 1 p.m.

Michael will eine Zigarette rauchen. Aber Nadine sagt ihm nein. Das Rauchen ist im Park nicht erlaubt.

Michael wants to smoke a cigarette. But Nadine tells him no. Smoking is not allowed in the park.

Nadine fragt ihre Kinder: „Wie gefällt es euch hier?"

Nadine asks her children: "How do you like it here?"

„Es macht so viel Spaß!", rufen Lea und Finn. Sie wollen nicht gehen.

"It's so much fun!", exclaim Lea and Finn. They don't want to leave.

Michael und Nadine lächeln. Sie sind froh, dass es den Kindern hier gefällt.

Michael and Nadine smile. They're happy that the kids love it here.

„Wer hat Lust auf Mittagessen?", fragt Nadine.

"Who wants to have lunch?", asks Nadine.

Alle sind hungrig. Sie setzen sich an einen Tisch und essen. Michael isst einen Burger. Nadine und die Kinder essen Eis, Würstchen und Kartoffeln.

Everyone is hungry. They sit at a table and eat. Michael has a burger. Nadine and the kids have ice cream, sausages, and potatoes.

Nach dem Mittagessen geht Michael zu einem Informationsschalter. „Können wir eine Karte haben?", fragt er. Die Karte zeigt alle Achterbahnen und mehr.

After lunch, Michael goes to an information desk. "Could we have a map?", he inquires. The maps shows all of the rollercoasters and more.

„Wohin sollen wir als Nächstes gehen?", fragt Nadine. Finn zeigt auf eine blaue Achterbahn. Lea will Karussell fahren. Michael möchte später Boot fahren. Es gibt so viel zu sehen. Die Eltern haben fast so viel Spaß wie die Kinder.

"Where should we go next?", asks Nadine. Finn points to a blue rollercoaster. Lea wants to go on the merry-go-round. Michael wants to ride the boat later. There is so much to see. The parents are having almost as much fun as the kids.

Es ist fast Sonnenuntergang. Der Tag ist endlich zu Ende. Sie machen ein paar Familienfotos. Der Europa-Park hat allen gefallen! Die Kinder wollen wiederkommen. „Bald sind Sommerferien," lacht Nadine.

It's almost sunset. The day has finally come to an end. They take some family photos. Everyone loved Europa Park! The kids want to come back again. "Summer vacation is coming soon!", laughs Nadine.

Chapter 7

"Christmas Cake" // "Weihnachtskuchen"

Photo of Black Forest Cherry Cake by Leonid Iastremskiy.

Featured Vocabulary

alle müssen nach Hause gehen: everyone has to return home, **aus der Tür**: out the door, **das nächste Weihnachten**: the next Christmas, **die Weihnachtsbaumleuchtung**: the Christmas tree lights, **draußen**: outside, **ein Buch über Island**: a book about Iceland, **ein Glas Wein**: a glass of wine, **ein Schokoladenkuchen**: a chocolate cake, **eine Schwarzwälder Kirschtorte**: a Black Forest cherry cake, **es ist Weihnachten**: it's Christmas, **festlich geschmückt**: festively decorated, **frischen Kirschen**: fresh cherries, **fröhlich**: happily, **ganz weiß**: all white, **heißen Kartoffeln**: hot potatoes, **in der Küche**: in the kitchen, **keinen solchen Kuchen**: no such cake, **kommt aus Island**: comes from Iceland, **Kuchenessen zu Weihnachten**: eating cake for Christmas, **liebt Schokolade**: loves chocolate, **magisch**: magical, **mit Schlagsahne**: with whipped cream, **natürlich**: of course, **neuere Tradition**: newer tradition, **Ritas Schwester**: Rita's sister, **schmeckt himmlisch**: tastes heavenly, **selbstgebackener Kuchen**: homemade cake, **sind da**: are there, **trotzdem**: regardless, **über alles Mögliche**: about all sorts of things, **unsicher**: unsure, **viele Geschenke**: many presents, **wieder zusammenkommen**: come together again, **zum Nachtisch**: for dessert

Short Story: "Christmas Cake"

Rita freut sich! Es ist Weihnachten und das ist ihr liebster Feiertag.

Rita is happy! It's Christmas and this is her favorite holiday.

Rita hat ihre Familie eingeladen. Ihre Großeltern Erwin und Magda sind da. Ihr Onkel Hallur ist auch zu Besuch. Er kommt aus Island. Ritas Schwester Antje ist mit ihrer Tochter Emma gekommen.

Rita has invited her family. Her grandparents, Erwin and Magda, are there. Her uncle, Hallur, is also visiting. He comes from Iceland. Rita's sister, Antje, has come with her daughter, Emma.

Rita kocht in der Küche. Sie bereitet Fisch mit Kartoffeln und Soße zu. Zum Nachtisch backt sie auch eine Schwarzwälder Kirschtorte. Dieser Kuchen ist einer ihrer Favoriten! Es ist ein Schokoladenkuchen mit Schlagsahne und frischen Kirschen.

Rita is cooking in the kitchen. She is preparing fish with potatoes and gravy. She is also baking a Black Forest cherry cake for dessert. This cake is one of her favorites! It's a chocolate cake with whipped cream and fresh cherries.

Das Haus ist festlich geschmückt. Draußen schneit es. Der Garten ist ganz weiß. Die kleine Emma erzählt vom Kindergarten. Onkel Hallur hört ihr zu, während er ein Glas Wein nippt.

The house is festively decorated. It's snowing outside. The garden is all white. Little Emma talks about kindergarten. Uncle Hallur listens to her while he sips a glass of wine.

Opa Erwin steht auf. „Ich werde die Weihnachtsbaumleuchtung anmachen", sagt er. „Mit Weihnachtsbeleuchtung sieht alles magisch aus!" Unter dem Baum liegen viele Geschenke. Die meisten sind für Emma.

Grandpa Erwin gets us. "I'm going to turn on the Christmas tree lights," he says. "Everything looks magical with Christmas lights!" There are many presents under the tree. Most of them are for Emma.

Emma plaudert weiter über alles Mögliche. „Meine Kindergärtnerin bekommt ein Baby", sagt sie. „Deshalb hat sie frei!"

Emma continues to chat about all sorts of things. "My kindergarten teacher is having a baby", she says. "That's why she's off from work!"

„Das ist besser so. Die Arbeit ist vielleicht zu anstrengend", antwortet Onkel Hallur. Emma nickt zustimmend.

"It's better that way. The work might be too strenuous," replies Uncle Hallur. Emma nods in agreement.

Rita bringt das Essen an den Tisch. Die heißen Kartoffeln und die Soße riechen sehr appetitlich.

Rita brings the food to the table. The hot potatoes and gravy smell quite appetizing.

„Rita, hast du das ganze Essen selbst gekauft? Es muss teuer gewesen sein!", ruft Antje.

"Rita, did you buy all of this food yourself? It must've been expensive!", exclaims Antje.

Rita schüttelt den Kopf und lächelt. „Es war kein Problem. Ich bin einfach froh, dass wir wieder zusammenkommen konnten!"

Rita shakes her head and smiles. "It was no problem. I'm just happy we could come together again!"

Bald sind alle mit dem Essen fertig. Onkel Hallur räumt den Tisch ab. Vor dem Nachtisch öffnet jeder seine Geschenke. Emma bekommt ein neues Puzzle. Opa Erwin bekommt von

Hallur ein Buch über Island.

Before long, eveyrone is finished eating. Uncle Hallur clears
the table. Everyone opens their presents before dessert. Emma
receives a new puzzle. Grandpa Erwin receives a book about
Iceland from Hallur.

**„Endlich ist es Zeit für die Schwarzwälder Kirschtorte", freut
sich Rita.**

"It's finally time for the Black Forest cherry cake," Rita says happily.

Jeder möchte ein Stück von Ritas Kuchen probieren.

Everyone wants to try a piece of Rita's cake.

**Nur Hallur ist unsicher. „Was ist das für ein Kuchen?", will er
wissen. Er hat noch nie von der Schwarzwälder Kirschtorte
gehört. In Island gibt es keinen solchen Kuchen.**

Only Hallur is unsure. "What kind of cake is that?", he wants to
know. He's·never heard of the Black Forest cherry cake. There's
no such cake in Iceland.

**Trotzdem probiert Hallur ein Stück vom Kuchen. Er strahlt.
Der erste Bissen schmeckt himmlisch!**

Regardless, Hallur tries a piece of the cake. He beams. The first bite tastes heavenly!

„Selbstgebackener Kuchen schmeckt am besten", sagt Oma Magda. „Er ist einfach so perfekt!"

"Homemade cake tastes the best," says Grandma Magda. "It's just so perfect!"

„Kuchenessen zu Weihnachten ist eine neuere Tradition," sagt Opa Erwin. Er fühlt sich ein wenig alt, ist aber auch sehr zufrieden.

"Eating cake for Christmas is a newer tradition," says Grandpa Erwin. He feels a little bit old but is also very satisfied.

Antje liebt Schokolade und liebt daher auch Schokoladenkuchen. Emma mag keine Schlagsahne, mag aber Kirschen.

Antje loves chocolate and thus also loves chocolate cake. Emma doesn't like whipped cream, but she likes cherries.

Bald ist die Nacht zu Ende und alle müssen nach Hause gehen. Viele schöne Erinnerungen wurden heute Abend geschaffen. Es war wirklich ein tolles Weihnachtsfest.

Soon, the night comes to an end and everyone has to return home. Many beautiful memories were created tonight. It was truly a great

Christmas celebration.

„Danke für so einen schönen Abend", sagt Onkel Hallur zu Rita. „Ich freue mich schon auf das nächste Weihnachten! Vielleicht gibt es ja wieder Schwarzwälder Kirschtorte?", lächelt er und geht aus der Tür.

"Thank you for such a lovely evening!" Uncle Hallur says to Rita. "I'm already looking forward to the next Christmas! Maybe there will be Black Forest cherry cake again?", he smiles and walks out the door.

Rita lacht fröhlich. „Ja, natürlich!"

Rita laughs happily. "Yes, of course!"

Chapter 8

"Springtime Meal" //
"Frühlingsessen"

Photo of asparagus with Black Forest ham by Darius Dzinnik.

Featured Vocabulary

an einen Tisch: at a table, **auf Wiedersehen**: goodbye, **das macht Sinn**: that makes sense, **das sehr leckere Essen**: the very delicious food, **der Kellner**: the server, **die Speisekarten**: the menus, **dieses Gericht**: this dish, **eigentlich**: actually, **ein bisschen**: a little bit, **ein Eis mit Obst**: an ice cream with fruit, **ein Gruß aus der Küche**: a greeting from the kitchen, **ein Projekt leiten**: manage a project, **eine Apfelschorle**: an apple spritzer, **etwas Brot und Butter**: some bread and butter, **Fabians Umzug**: Fabian's move, **gute Freunde**: good friends, **hell wie der Tag**: as bright as day, **heute Abend**: tonight, **ich würde lieber**: I'd rather, **im Frühjahr**: in the spring, **im selben Lokal**: at the same eatery, **in Deutschland bleiben**: stay in Germany, **in Winternächten**: on winter nights, **ins Ausland**: abroad, **keinen anderen Weg**: no other way, **köstlich**: delectable, **mein Chef**: my boss, **nach Schweden umziehen**: move to Sweden, **nächstes Mal**: next time, **nicht schlecht**: not bad, **nicht wohl**: not well, **Sauce Hollandaise**: Hollandaise sauce, **so weit wegziehen**: move so far away, **Spargelsaison**: asparagus season, **viel wärmer**: much warmer, **wegen meines Jobs**: because of my job, **weißer Spargel mit Schwarzwälder Schinken**: white asparagus with Black Forest ham, **zum Glück**: fortunately

Short Story: "Springtime Meal"

Kai und Fabian sind gute Freunde. Sie essen oft zusammen im selben Lokal.

Kai and Fabian are good friends. They often eat together at the same eatery.

Heute Abend hat das Lokal ein besonderes Angebot: Weißer Spargel mit Schwarzwälder Schinken, Kartoffeln und Sauce Hollandaise! Dieses Gericht wird nur während der Spargelsaison im Frühjahr serviert.

Tonight, the eatery has a special offering: white asparagus with Black Forest ham, potatoes, and Hollandaise sauce! This dish is only served during the asparagus season in the springtime.

Sie setzen sich an einen Tisch und der Kellner bringt die Speisekarten. „Was möchten Sie trinken?", fragt er.

They seat themselves at a table and the server brings the menus. "What would you like to drink?", he asks.

„Ich nehme eine Apfelschorle", antwortet Fabian. Kai nimmt auch die Apfelschorle.

"I'll take an apple spritzer," replies Fabian. Kai also takes the apple spritzer.

Fabian sieht nicht glücklich aus. Kai befragt ihn dazu. „Was ist los, Fabian? Fühlst du dich nicht wohl?"

Fabian doesn't look happy. Kai asks him about it. "What's the matter, Fabian? Are you not feeling well?"

Fabian schüttelt den Kopf. „Nein, eigentlich nicht."

Fabian shakes his head. "No, actually not."

„Was ist das Problem?"

"What's the problem?"

„Es ist wegen meines Jobs. Ich bekomme einen neuen Arbeitsplatz."

"It's because of my job. I'm receiving a new workplace."

„Wo musst du hingehen?", fragt Kai.

"Where must you go to?", asks Kai.

„Ins Ausland. Ich muss bald nach Schweden umziehen", erklärt Fabian. „Mein Chef, Herr Meier, will es so."

"Abroad. I have to move to Sweden soon," explains Fabian. "My boss, Mr. Meier, wants it that way."

Kai will nicht, dass Fabian ins Ausland zieht. „Warum musst du so weit wegziehen? Kannst du nicht in Deutschland bleiben?"

Kai doesn't want Fabian to move abroad. "Why do you have to move so far away? Can't you stay in Germany?"

„Ich muss dort ein Projekt leiten", sagt Fabian. „Es gibt keinen anderen Weg."

"I have to manage a project there," says Fabian. "There is no other way."

„Ich denke, das macht Sinn. Vielleicht gefällt dir dein neuer Job dort sogar!", sagt Kai.

"I suppose that makes sense. Maybe you'll even like your new job there!", says Kai.

Fabian gluckst. „Ja, vielleicht. Schweden ist nicht schlecht. Aber ich würde lieber nach Spanien gehen. Da ist es viel wärmer. Und das Essen ist so lecker!"

Fabian chuckles. "Yeah, maybe. Sweden isn't bad. But I'd rather go to Spain. It's much warmer there. And the food is so delicious!"

Der Kellner kommt wieder. Er hat die Getränke dabei. Und er hat etwas Brot und Butter mitgebracht. „Das ist ein Gruß aus

der Küche", sagt er. „Was möchten Sie essen?"

The waiter comes back. He has the drinks with him. And he has brought some bread and butter. "This is a greeting from the kitchen," he says. "What would you like to eat?"

Kai beginnt. „Also, ich nehme den Spargel mit Schwarzwälder Schinken und Kartoffeln. Und ein bisschen von der Sauce."

Kai starts. "So, I'll take the asparagus with Black Forest ham and potatoes. And a little bit of the sauce."

Der Kellner nickt und lächelt. „Ja, natürlich."

The waiter nods and smiles. "Yes, of course."

„Ich nehme auch den weißen Spargel mit Schinken, Kartoffeln und Sauce Hollandaise. Und zum Nachtisch ein Eis mit Obst", sagt Fabian.

"I'll also take the white asparagus with ham, potatoes, and Hollandaise sauce. And an ice cream with fruit for dessert," says Fabian.

Jetzt warten sie, während die Küche ihre Bestellungen vorbereitet. Fabian spricht wieder über Schweden. „Dort ist es sehr kalt. Und in Winternächten ist es hell wie der Tag!"

Now they wait while the kitchen prepares their orders. Fabian talks about Sweden again. "It's very cold there. And on winter nights, it's as bright as day!"

„Spanien ist wirklich besser! Aber du bist gut in deinem Job. Daran glaube ich,“ sagt Kai.

"Spain really is better! But you're good at your job. I believe in that," says Kai.

Fabian ist begeistert. „Danke“, sagt er. „Du bist ein toller Freund!“

Fabian is delighted. "Thanks," he says. "You're a great friend!"

Endlich ist das Essen da. Es sieht köstlich aus. Die drei Spargelstangen sind riesig. Die Kartoffeln und der Schwarzwälder Schinken riechen sehr würzig und appetitlich. Und es schmeckt himmlisch! Die Sauce Hollandaise rundet alles perfekt ab. Kai und Fabian sind zufrieden.

The food finally arrives. It looks delectable. The three asparagus spears are huge. The potatoes and Black Forest ham smell very spicy and appetizing. And it tastes heavenly! The Hollandaise sauce rounds everything off perfectly. Kai and Fabian are satisfied.

Fabian isst sein Eis mit Obst. Kai trinkt eine Tasse deutschen

Mokka. Er ist nicht so hungrig wie Fabian.

Fabian eats his ice cream with fruit. Kai drinks a cup of German mocha. He isn't as hungry as Fabian.

Die beiden Freunde unterhalten sich weiter über Fabians Umzug nach Schweden. Fabian muss zum Glück nicht sehr lange in Schweden bleiben. Er wird bald wieder in Deutschland sein. Natürlich werden sie wieder hier essen!

The two friends talk some more about Fabian's move to Sweden. Fortunately, Fabian doesn't have to stay in Sweden for very long. He will be back in Germany soon. Of course, they will eat here again!

Der Kellner bringt die Rechnung. Kai will das Essen bezahlen. „Darf ich dich zum Essen einladen?", fragt er Fabian.

The waiter brings the bill. Kai wants to pay for the meal. "May I treat you to dinner?", he asks Fabian.

„Vielen Dank! Nächstes Mal lade ich dich ein", verspricht Fabian.

"Thanks a lot! I'll treat you next time," promises Fabian.

Der Kellner lächelt freundlich und sagt: „Auf Wiedersehen!"

The waiter makes a friendly smile and says, "Goodbye!"

Sie verlassen das Lokal. Es regnet. Sie haben keinen Regenschirm. Aber alles ist gut. Kai und Fabian freuen sich über ihre Freundschaft und das sehr leckere Essen!

They leave the eatery. It's raining. They don't have an umbrella. But, everything is fine. Kai and Fabian are happy about their friendship and the very delicious food!

Chapter 9

"Butter Pretzel" // "Butterbrezel"

Photo of German pretzel with butter by Evgenija Lanz.

Featured Vocabulary

aktuell arbeitslos: currently unemployed, **auf ein Sofa**: on a sofa, **bestimmte Papiere**: certain papers, **bitte**: please, **das heutige Datum**: today's date, **dauert nicht lange**: doesn't take long, **der Tür dort drüben**: the door over there, **ein junger Mann**: a young man, **ein Praktikum**: an internship, **ein Vorstellungsgespräch**: a job interview, **eine Bewerbung**: a job application, **eine Brille**: a pair of glasses, **eine Stellenanzeige**: a job advertisement, **eine Tasse Tee**: a cup of tea, **einen neuen Kurs machen**: take a new course, **gleich zu meinem Kollegen**: straight to my colleague, **guten Tag**: good day, **hallo**: hello, **ich schaffe das**: I can do it, **ihre Miete bezahlen**: pay her rent, **im vierten Stock**: on the fourth floor, **in die Stadt**: into the city, **in Eile**: in a hurry, **klopft an der Tür**: knocks on the door, **kurze Haare**: short hair, **Lebenslauf**: curriculum vitae, **Lebensmittel einkaufen**: buy groceries, **mein Beruf**: my profession, **nach oben**: to the top, **nächste Woche**: next week, **nicht nötig**: not necessary, **nichts**: nothing, **noch auf**: still open, **noch eine Frage**: another question, **schon zu**: already closed, **und so weiter**: and so on, **viel aufschreiben**: write a lot of things down, **völlig in Ordnung**: perfectly fine, **wieder**: again, **zu dem salzigen Teig**: with the salty dough

Short Story: "Butter Pretzel"

Katharina ist aktuell arbeitslos. Sie sieht im Internet eine Stellenanzeige für ein Unternehmen.

Katharina is currently unemployed. She sees a job advertisement for a company online.

Katharina muss Geld verdienen. Sie muss ihre Miete bezahlen und Lebensmittel einkaufen.

Katharina needs to earn money. She has to pay her rent and buy groceries.

Sie hat online eine Bewerbung ausgefüllt. Sie hat heute ein Vorstellungsgespräch bei dem Unternehmen. Dafür braucht sie bestimmte Papiere.

She has filled out a job application online. She has a job interview at the company today. She needs certain papers for this.

Sie fährt mit dem Fahrrad in die Stadt. Sie ist in Eile und stürzt fast! Zum Glück passiert nichts.

She rides her bicycle into the city. She's in a hurry and almost crashes! Luckily, nothing happens.

Das Unternehmen hat ein Büro mitten in der Stadt. Es ist im vierten Stock.

The company has an office in the middle of the city. It's on the fourth floor.

Katharina fährt mit dem Aufzug nach oben. An der Tür hängt ein Schild. In großen Buchstaben steht dort „Anmeldung zum Vorstellungsgespräch". Ein Pfeil darunter zeigt auf einem Raum.

Katharina takes the elevator to the top. A sign hangs on the door. It says there, "Registration for the job interview," in large letters. An arrow below it points to a room.

Katharina klopft an der Tür. Sie ist aufgeregt.

Katharina knocks on the door. She is excited.

Ein Beamter begrüßt sie. „Guten Tag", sagt er.

A clerk greets her. "Good day," he says.

„Hallo, ich habe einen Termin. Ich habe eine Bewerbung geschrieben. Heute ist mein Vorstellungsgespräch", sagt Katharina.

"Hello, I have an appointment. I've written a job application. Today is my job interview," says Katharina.

„Das freut mich! Darf ich Sie bitten, dieses Formular auszufüllen?" Der Beamte gibt ihr ein Blatt Papier. „Im Anschluss ist das Vorstellungsgespräch. Brauchen Sie Hilfe?"

"I'm pleased to hear that! May I ask you to fill out this form?" The clerk gives her a sheet of paper. "This is followed by the job interview. Do you need assistance?"

„Nein, danke. Ich schaffe das", antwortet Katharina.

"No, thank you. I can do it," replies Katharina.

Katharina setzt sich auf ein Sofa im Raum und kreuzt Fragen an. Sie muss viel aufschreiben. Ihren Familiennamen, Familienstand, das heutige Datum und so weiter. Dann bringt sie das Formular zurück zu dem Beamten.

Katharina sits down on a sofa in the room and checks off questions. She has to write a lot of things down. Her surname, marital status, today's date, and so on. Then she brings the form back to the clerk.

„Sehr gut. Ich schicke Sie gleich zu meinem Kollegen. Er leitet das Vorstellungsgespräch."

"Very good. I'm sending you straight to my colleague. He's leading the job interview."

„Wohin soll ich gehen?"

"Where shall I go to?"

Der Beamte zeigt den Weg. „Zu der Tür dort drüben."

The clerk shows the way. "To the door over there."

In dem anderen Zimmer sitzt ein junger Mann. Er hat kurze Haare und eine Brille.

A young man is sitting in the other room. He has short hair and a pair of glasses.

„Hallo", sagt er. „Haben Sie Ihre Papiere dabei?"

"Hello," he says. "Do you have your papers with you?"

Katharina übergibt ein paar Blätter Papier. Sie hat bereits ihr Schulzeugnis und ihren Lebenslauf per E-Mail geschickt.

Katharina hands over a few sheets of paper. She has already emailed her school certificate and curriculum vitae.

Der junge Mann lächelt. „Perfekt. Fangen wir an!"

The young man smiles. "Perfect. Let's get started!"

Das Gespräch verläuft sehr gut. Katharina fühlt sich wohl. Sie

hofft, dass sie eingestellt wird.

The conversation goes very well. Katharina feels comfortable. She hopes she will be hired!

„Ich habe noch eine Frage", sagt Katharina. „Mein Beruf ist Bürokauffrau. Müsste ich einen neuen Kurs machen?"

"I have another question," says Katharina. My profession is as office administrator. Would I need to take a new course?"

„Nein, das ist nicht nötig", sagt der Mann. „Ihr alter Beruf ist völlig in Ordnung! Es wird ein Praktikum geben. Aber das dauert nicht lange. Ich rufe Sie an, wann Sie mit der Arbeit beginnen können."

"No, that isn't necessary," says the man. "Your old profession is perfectly fine! There will be an internship. But that doesn't take long. I'll call you when you can begin work."

„Vielen Dank!", sagt Katharina.

"Thank you very much!", says Katharina.

„Wir schicken Ihnen den Vertrag nächste Woche", sagt der Mann. „Bitte unterschreiben Sie ganz unten."

We'll send you the contract next week," says the man. "Please sign at the very bottom."

Katharina ist sehr glücklich! Sie will sich belohnen. Sie möchte eine leckere Butterbrezel kaufen. Das isst sie sehr gerne! Viele Geschäfte sind schon zu. Aber die Bäckerei ist noch auf. Katharina holt sich zur Brezel eine Tasse Tee.

Katharina is very happy! She wants to reward herself. She would like to buy a delicious butter pretzel. She loves eating them! Many stores are already closed. But the bakery is still open. Katharina gets herself a cup of tea to go with the pretzel.

In der Nähe ist ein Park. Sie setzt sich auf eine Bank. Katharina freut sich über das Unternehmen. Bald wird sie wieder einen Job haben. Dann kann sie mehr Dinge genießen.

There is a park nearby. She sits down on a bench. Katharina is happy about the company. Soon she will have a job again. Then she can enjoy more things.

Sie isst die Brezel. Die Butter passt perfekt zu dem salzigen Teig. Es ist nichts Besonderes, aber trotzdem sehr lecker! Sie schmecken am besten nach einem aufregenden Tag.

She eats the pretzel. The butter goes perfectly with the salty dough. It's nothing special, but still very tasty! They taste best after an exciting day.

Chapter 10

"Doctor's Advice" // "Rat eines Arztes"

Photo of Triberg path by Matyas Rehak.

Featured Vocabulary

an einer Straßenecke: on a street corner, **aus dem Autofenster**: from the car window, **das Unwohlsein**: the malaise, **der Eingang zur Arztpraxis**: the entrance to the doctor's office, **die Arzthelferin**: the doctor's assistant, **die notwendigen persönlichen Daten**: the necessary personal data, **dieses Mal**: this time, **ein alter Bekannter**: an old acquaintance, **ein bestimmter Ort**: a particular place, **ein Formular**: a form, **einen Vorschlag**: a proposal, **erstaunlich**: amazing, **etwas Schlimmes**: something bad, **ganz Besonderes**: very special, **ganz gesund**: quite healthy, **geht hinein**: walks in, **Horsts Fuß**: Horst's foot, **kein Wunder**: no wonder, **mit einem Fenster**: with a window, **nach Triberg**: to Triberg, **nicht leicht**: not easy, **niemand antwortet**: nobody answers, **sehr sauber**: very clean, **seine Symptome**: his symptoms, **so müde**: so tired, **unvergesslich**: memorable, **viel besser**: much better, **vollständige körperliche Untersuchung**: full physical examination, **vor drei Wochen**: three weeks ago, **wahrscheinlich der Grund**: probably the reason, **was für eine Freude**: what a pleasure, **weiß nicht warum**: doesn't know why, **wenig Energie**: little energy, **zum ersten Mal**: for the first time

Short Story: "Doctor's Advice"

Horst fühlt sich nicht wohl. Aber er weiß nicht warum.

Horst doesn't feel well. But he doesn't know why.

Er will zu seinem Arzt gehen. Er ist ein alter Bekannter. Horst ruft an, aber niemand antwortet.

He wants to go see his doctor. He is an old acquaintance. Horst calls, but nobody answers.

Horst ruft ein Taxi. Er fährt in die Stadt zum Arzt. Der Fahrer unterhält sich gerne. Horst schaut aus dem Autofenster. Es ist Sommer und viele Menschen entspannen sich draußen.

Horst calls a cab. He rides into town to the doctor. The driver enjoys chatting. Horst looks out from the car window. It's summer and many people are relaxing outside.

Der Eingang zur Arztpraxis liegt an einer Straßenecke. Horst geht hinein und meldet sich an der Rezeption an.

The entrance to the doctor's office is on a street corner. Horst walks in and registers with the reception desk.

„Guten Tag", sagt Horst.

"Good day," says Horst.

Die Arzthelferin begrüßt ihn. „Guten Tag. Wie können wir Ihnen heute helfen?", fragt sie.

The doctor's assistant greets him. "How can we help you today?", she asks.

„Ich würde gerne Doktor Haller sehen. Mir geht es nicht gut," erklärt Horst.

"I'd like to see Doctor Haller. I haven't been feeling well," Horst explains.

„Sicher. Sie müssen nur das hier ausfüllen." Sie gibt Horst ein Formular. „Schreiben Sie bitte Ihr Geburtsjahr und Ihren Geburtsort auf. Was ist Ihr Beruf?"

"Sure. You'll just need to complete this." She gives Horst a form. "Please write down your birth year and place of birth. What is your occupation?"

„Ich arbeite nicht mehr", sagt Horst. Er gibt die notwendigen persönlichen Daten an. Horst fällt auf, dass die Arztpraxis innen sehr sauber ist.

"I don't work anymore," says Horst. He provides the necessary personal data. Horst notices that the doctor's office is very clean inside.

Die Arzthelferin liest das Formular durch. „Das Formular sieht gut aus. Bitte kommen Sie hier entlang zu Doktor Haller," sagt sie.

The doctor's assistant reads over the form. "The form looks good. Please come this way to see Doctor Haller," she says.

Sie gehen den Flur entlang in einem Raum mit einem Fenster. Doktor Haller wartet drinnen. Er ist froh, Horst wiederzusehen.

They walk down the hallway into a room with a window. Doctor Haller is waiting inside. He is happy to see Horst again.

„Lieber Horst! Was für eine Freude, dich zu sehen. Wie ist das Leben so?"

"Dear Horst! What a pleasure to see you. How has life been?"

„Das Leben ist gut", antwortet Horst. „Ich fühle mich nur gerade unwohl."

"Life is good," Horst replies. "I'm just feeling unwell now."

„Was meinst du damit?", fragt Doktor Haller.

"What do you mean by that?", asks Doctor Haller.

Horst erklärt seine Symptome. „Ich schlafe viel, habe aber wenig Energie. Ich bleibe einfach in meiner Wohnung. Außerdem habe ich Fieber."

Horst explains his symptoms. "I'm sleeping a lot but have little energy. I'm just staying inside my apartment. I'm also feverish."

„Mal sehen, was ich finden kann", antwortet Doktor Haller. Er führt eine vollständige körperliche Untersuchung durch.

"Let me see what I can find," replies Doctor Haller. He does a complete physical examination.

Er stellt fest, dass Horst eigentlich ganz gesund ist. Auch seine Temperatur ist fast normal. Das Unwohlsein hat eine tiefer liegende Ursache.

He finds that Horst is actually quite healthy. His temperature is also almost normal. The malaise is rooted in something deeper.

„Horst, du bist ganz gesund", sagt Doktor Haller. „Ist etwas Schlimmes passiert?"

"Horst, you are quite healthy," says Doctor Haller. "Has something bad happened?"

Horst nickt. „Ja, meine Frau ist vor drei Wochen gestorben. Sie war etwas ganz Besonderes für mich."

Horst nods. "Yes, my wife died three weeks ago. She was very special to me."

„Es tut mir leid, das zu hören. Es ist nicht leicht, einen geliebten Menschen zu verlieren. Aber das ist wahrscheinlich der Grund, warum du so müde bist!"

"I'm sorry to hear that. It's not easy to lose a loved one. But this is probably the reason why you are so tired!"

„Was ist jetzt am besten zu tun?"

"What is the best thing to do now?"

„Hat Ihrer Frau ein bestimmter Ort gefallen?"

"Did your wife like a particular place?"

„Ja, das hat sie!", lacht Horst. „Sie liebte das Schwarzwaldmuseum in Triberg."

"Yes, she did!", laughs Horst. "She loved the Black Forest Museum in Triberg."

Doktor Haller denkt tief nach. „Wenn das so ist, habe ich einen Vorschlag. Versuchen Sie, diesen besonderen Ort zu besuchen, wenn Sie die Kraft dazu haben. Ich empfehle es sehr!"

Doctor Haller thinks deeply. "In that case, I have a proposal. Try to visit this special place when you have the strength. I highly recommend it!"

Horst gefällt die Idee. Die Reise soll unvergesslich und gut für seine Gesundheit sein. Er bedankt sich bei Doktor Haller für den guten Rat und fährt nach Hause.

Horst likes the idea. The trip should be memorable and good for his health. He thanks Doctor Haller for the great advice and goes back home.

Am nächsten Tag reist er nach Triberg. Horst besucht zum ersten Mal das Schwarzwaldmuseum. Es ist erstaunlich! Kein Wunder, dass es seiner Frau gifiel. Horst fühlt sich sofort viel besser.

The next day, he travels to Triberg. Horst visits the Black Forest Museum for the first time. It's amazing! No wonder his wife liked it. Horst immediately feels much better.

Horst reist noch vor Sonnenuntergang nach Hause. Er hatte einen schönen Tag! Er möchte auch an andere Orte reisen, die seiner Frau gefallen haben.

Horst travels back home before sunset. He had a good day! He also wants to travel to other places his wife enjoyed.

Aber jetzt tut Horsts Fuß weh. Er muss noch einmal zu Doktor Haller gehen. Aber dieses Mal weiß er, was das Problem ist!

But now Horst's foot hurts. He needs to see Doctor Haller again. But this time he knows what the problem is!

Chapter 11

"Field Trip to the Mine" // "Ausflug ins Bergwerk"

Photo of a mine by Tomas Sereda.

Featured Vocabulary

am Eingang: at the entrance, **am Freiburger Bahnhof**: at Freiburg Station, **bis zum Abend geöffnet**: open until the evening, **bis zur Schließzeit**: until the closing time, **dauert zwei Stunden**: lasts two hours, **der Ausflug**: the field trip, **die Arbeit**: the work, **die ganze Klasse**: the whole class, **ein Foto von uns**: a photo of us, **ein großes Abenteuer**: a great adventure, **ein Kind und seine Eltern**: a child and his parents, **eine Führung**: a guided tour, **eine Stunde später**: an hour later, **Entschuldigung**: excuse me, **fast Nacht**: almost nighttime, **gehen zusammen**: go together, **ich will**: I want to, **kein Problem**: no problem, **keine Hausaufgaben**: no homework, **keineswegs gewöhnlich**: by no means ordinary, **Klassenkameraden**: classmates, **meine Geschwister**: my siblings, **mit dem Zug**: by train, **noch mehr zu entdecken**: still more to discover, **nur Wände aus Stein**: only walls of stone, **pünktlich**: on time, **recht günstig**: quite affordable, **sehr müde**: very tired, **tief in die Erde**: deep into the earth, **um 8 Uhr morgens**: at 8 a.m., **über etwas anderes**: about something else, **viele Treppen**: many stairs, **viele verschiedene Dinge**: many different things, **winkt zum Abschied**: waves goodbye

Short Story: "Field Trip to the Mine"

Sina und ihre Klassenkameraden machen heute einen Ausflug. Sie gehen in das Museums-Bergwerk Schauinsland. Der Schauinsland ist ein Berg in der Nähe der Stadt Freiburg.

Sina and her classmates are going on a field trip today. They are going to the Schauinsland Mining Museum. The Schauinsland is a mountain near the city of Freiburg.

Sie fahren mit dem Zug. Die Abfahrt vom Bahnsteig erfolgt um 8 Uhr morgens. Eine Durchsage ertönt. Der Zug ist pünktlich.

They are traveling by train. Departure from the platform is at 8 a.m. An announcement sounds. The train is on time.

Eine Stunde später kommt er am Freiburger Bahnhof an. Sina ist schon aufgeregt! Sie war noch nie in einem Bergwerk. Sie hat nur in Büchern darüber gelesen.

It arrives at Freiburg Station an hour later. Sina is already excited! She has never been to a mine before. She has only read books about them.

Das Museum liegt direkt unter dem Berg. Der Eintritt ist recht günstig.

The museum is located directly under the mountain. Admission is quite affordable.

Die Klasse bekommt eine Führung. Ihr Lehrer hat das für sie organisiert.

The class gets a guided tour. Their teacher has organized it for them.

Sie beginnt am Eingang. Dort geben sie ihre Taschen ab. Danach erhält die Klasse gelbe Helme.

It starts at the entrance. They hand in their bags there. Thereafter, the class is given yellow helmets.

Das Museum ist keineswegs gewöhnlich. Es ist ein altes Bergwerk. Früher haben hier Menschen gearbeitet. Und sie trugen auch Helme.

The museum is by no means ordinary. It's an old mine. People used to work here. And they also wore helmets.

Die Führerin erklärt viele verschiedene Dinge. Sie kennt sich sehr gut aus. „Vorsicht, bitte! Ihr müsst aufpassen, dass ihr nicht stürzt", sagt sie.

The guide explains many different things. She knows her way around very well. "Careful, please! You have to pay attention so that you don't fall," she says.

Sina kann sich vorstellen, dass die Arbeit damals anstrengend war. Links und rechts gibt es nur Wände aus Stein.

Sina can imagine that the work back then was exhausting. There are only walls of stone to the left and right.

Sinas Freundin Michaela ist nicht glücklich. „Ich will nach Hause," sagt sie.

Sina's friend, Michaela, is not happy. "I want to go home," she says.

„Warum?", fragt Sina.

"Why?", asks Sina.

„Der Ausflug ist langweilig!", ruft Michaela. „Meine Geschwister haben viel coolere Orte besucht."

"The field trip is boring!", says Michaela. "My siblings visited much cooler places."

Sina versteht Michaela nicht. Sie freut sich, neue Dinge zu lernen. „Es ist so toll hier!"

Sina doesn't understand Michaela. She's happy to learn new things. "It's so awesome here!"

Die Führung dauert zwei Stunden.

The guided tour lasts two hours.

Der Lehrer sagt dann: „Jeder sucht sich einen Partner oder eine Partnerin. Ihr könnt zusammen das Museum besichtigen."

The teacher then says, "Everyone, find a (male or female) partner. You can tour the museum together."

Sina und Michaela gehen zusammen. Sie schauen sich alles an.

Sina and Michaela go together. They look at everything.

Das Bergwerk geht tief in die Erde. Sina und Michaela steigen viele Treppen hinunter.

The mine goes deep into the earth. Sina and Michaela climb down many stairs.

Unten ist es besonders leise. Sina kann ihre Klasse kaum hören. Sie fahren mit einem kleinen Zug. Eine paar andere Schüler fahren auch mit.

It's particularly quiet down below. Sina can hardly hear her class. There are still old machines around. They ride a little train. A few other students also ride with them.

Nach der Zugfahrt stehen ein Kind und seine Eltern neben Sina und Michaela. Die Frau fragt Sina: „Entschuldigung, könnten Sie bitte ein Foto von uns machen?"

After the train ride, a child and his parents are standing next to Sina and Michaela. The woman asks Sina, "Excuse me, could you please take a photo of us?"

„Das ist kein Problem!", sagt Sina. Sie macht mehrere Fotos hintereinander.

"That's no problem!", says Sina. She takes several photos in a row.

„Vielen Dank!", sagt die Familie gemeinsam.

"Thank you very much!", the family says together as one.

Das Bergwerk-Museum ist bis zum Abend geöffnet. Sina und ihre Klasse bleiben bis zur Schließzeit.

The Mining Museum is open until the evening. Sina and her class stay until the closing time.

Sie treffen sich am Eingang wieder, bevor sie gehen. Die Führerin winkt zum Abschied.

They reunite at the entrance before leaving. The guide waves goodbye.

„Danke!", sagt die ganze Klasse zu ihr.

"Thank you!", the whole class says to her.

Sina ist sehr müde. Es ist fast Nacht. Aber heute war ein großes Abenteuer. Sie möchte wieder ins Museum gehen. Es gibt noch mehr zu entdecken. Und sie freut sich auch über etwas anderes. Heute gibt es keine Hausaufgaben!

Sina is very tired. It's almost nighttime. But today was a great adventure. She wants to go back to the museum again. There is still more to discover. And she is also happy about something else. There is no homework today!

Chapter 12

"The World's Biggest Cuckoo Clock" // "Die Größte Kuckucksuhr der Welt"

Photo of World's Biggest Cuckoo Clock by Michiel Klootwijk.

Featured Vocabulary

aus Wales im Vereinigten Königreich: from Wales in the United Kingdom, **Briefmarken mit Kuckucksuhren**: postage stamps featuring cuckoo clocks, **bunte Blumen**: colorful flowers, **die größte Kuckucksuhr der Welt**: the biggest cuckoo clock in the world, **die Luft**: the air, **die Schüler**: the students, **ein Getränk aus einem Automaten**: a drink from a vending machine, **eine kleine Stadt**: a small town, **eine Oase der Natur**: an oasis of nature, **er ist vorbereitet**: he is prepared, **erste Mal**: first time, **fassungslos**: stunned, **für die Sinne**: for the senses, **klingt wirklich interessant**: sounds really interesting, **Kuckucksuhrensammler**: cuckoo clock collectors, **mit einem anderen männlichen Studenten**: with another male student, **miteinander**: with each other, **nickt zustimmend**: nods in agreement, **plötzlich**: suddenly, **schwer zu reparieren**: difficult to repair, **sehr unterhaltsam**: very entertaining, **sie übernachten**: they stay overnight, **so groß wie ein Haus**: as big as a house, **so viel wie möglich**: as much as possible, **über den Schwarzwald**: about the Black Forest, **über sein besonderes Abenteuer**: about his special adventure, **verschiedene Fotos**: various photos, **viele Holzfiguren**: many wooden figures, **wie schwer und groß**: how heavy and big

Short Story: "The World's Biggest Cuckoo Clock"

James ist Schüler eines Gymnasiums. Sie lernen gerade über den Schwarzwald.

James is a student at a high school. They are now learning about the Black Forest.

James und seine Klasse machen einen Ausflug nach Schonach. Es ist eine kleine Stadt. In Schonach gibt es auch die größte Kuckucksuhr der Welt.

James and his class are going on a field trip to Schonach. It a small town. Schonach is also home to the biggest cuckoo clock in the world!

Die Schüler fahren mit dem Bus nach Schonach. James ist aufgeregt. Es ist ein heißer Tag heute. Er ist vorbereitet und hat ein Getränk aus einem Automaten dabei.

The students ride a bus to Schonach. James is excited. It's a hot day today. He is prepared and has a drink from a vending machine with him.

James hat eine gute Freundin namens Julia. Sie spielen oft

zusammen Fußball.

James has a good friend by the name of Julia. They often play soccer together.

„Bist du das erste Mal in Schonach?", fragt James.

"Is this your first time to Schonach?", asks James.

„Ja, ich bin das erste Mal dort," antwortet Julia.

"Yes, it's my first time there," replies Julia.

„Die Luft ist so schön," sagt James. Er ist ein Austauschstudent aus Wales im Vereinigten Königreich. Er möchte so viel wie möglich über den Schwarzwald lernen.

"The air is so lovely," says James. He is an exchange student from Wales in the United Kingdom. He wants to learn as much as he can about the Black Forest.

Julia lächelt und nickt zustimmend. „Der Schwarzwald ist eine Oase der Natur. Das ist sehr inspirierend für die Sinne."

Julia smiles and nods in agreement. "The Black Forest is an oasis of nature. It's very inspiring for the senses."

Bald kommen sie in Schonach an. Die ganze Klasse geht durch die Stadt. James und Julia reden weiter miteinander.

They soon arrive in Schonach. The entire class walks through the town. James and Julia continue talking to each other.

„Haben viele Menschen in Deutschland Kuckucksuhren?", fragt James.

"Do many people have cuckoo clocks in Germany?", asks James.

„Ältere Menschen scheinen sie besonders zu mögen. Meine Großmutter hat einen zu Hause. Sie liebt es, sie jeden Tag zu hören. Es gibt auch Clubs für Kuckucksuhrensammler!", sagt Julia.

"Older people seem to like them in particular. My grandma has one at her home. She loves hearing it everyday. There are clubs for cuckoo clock collectors too!", says Julia.

„Wow, das klingt wirklich interessant!", antwortet James.

"Wow, that sounds really interesting!", replies James.

Schließlich kommen sie bei der größten Kuckucksuhr der Welt an. James ist fassungslos.

They finally arrive at the world's biggest cuckoo clock. James is stunned.

Diese Kuckucksuhr ist so groß wie ein Haus. Im Garten vor

der gigantischen Uhr stehen viele Holzfiguren. Überall blühen bunte Blumen. Die Klasse wird immer aufgeregter.

The cuckoo clock is as big as a house. There are many wooden figures in the garden in front of the gigantic clock. Colorful flowers are blooming everywhere. The class is growing more excited.

Plötzlich läutet die Kuckucksuhr. Tanzende Holzfiguren tauchen vom Balkon der Uhr auf. Es ist ein magisches Spektakel.

Suddenly, the cuckoo clock chimes. Dancing wooden figures emerge from the balcony of the clock. It's a magical spectacle.

James geht um die größte Kuckucksuhr der Welt herum. Julia kommt mit. Sie macht verschiedene Fotos von der Uhr.

James walks around the world's biggest cuckoo clock. Julia comes along. She takes various photos of the clock.

„Wie schwer und groß ist diese Uhr?", fragt James. „Sie sieht schwer zu reparieren aus."

"How heavy and big is this clock?", asks James. "It looks difficult to repair."

„Es dauert wahrscheinlich sehr lange, diese Uhr zu reparieren," sagt Julia.

"It probably takes a really long time to fix this clock," says Julia.

In der Nähe gibt es eine Broschüre über die Kuckucksuhr. James nimmt eine mit, um sie später zu studieren.

There is a brochure about the cuckoo clock closeby. James takes one with him to study later.

Sie übernachten in einem Hotel in Schonach. James bekommt ein Doppelzimmer mit einem anderen männlichen Studenten.

They stay overnight at a hotel in Schonach. James gets a double room with another male student.

Im Hotel nimmt James zunächst eine Dusche. Dann liest er die Broschüre über die Kuckucksuhr. Das ist sehr unterhaltsam! Er hat auch Briefmarken mit Kuckucksuhren gekauft, um sie als Souvenir mitzubringen. James könnte nicht glücklicher sein über sein besonderes Abenteuer im Schwarzwald.

At the hotel, James first takes a shower. Then, he reads the brochure about the cuckoo clock. It's very entertaining! He also bought postage stamps featuring cuckoo clocks to bring back as souvenirs. James couldn't be happier about his special adventure in the Black Forest.

Chapter 13

"Kaiserstuhl Vineyards" // "Kaiserstuhl Weinberge"

Photo of Kaiserstuhl vineyard by Peter Eckert.

Featured Vocabulary

alles Gute für die Reise: all the best for the trip, **am frühen Nachmittag**: in the early afternoon, **am Meer**: by the sea, **am nächsten Morgen**: the next morning, **an ihrem letzten Tag**: on her last day, **bunte und duftende Weintrauben**: colorful and fragrant wine grapes, **die berühmten Rotweine**: the famous red wines, **die grünen Hügel**: the verdant hills, **die meisten Deutschen**: most Germans, **ein bisschen teuer**: a little expensive, **ein Dutzend Flaschen**: a dozen bottles, **ein entspanntes Mittagessen**: a relaxing lunch, **eine Busstunde**: an hour by bus, **einige Deutsche**: some Germans, **etwas anderes**: something different, **hoch über den Wolken**: high above the clouds, **Hunderte Fotos der Weinberge**: hundreds of photos of the vineyards, **in ein paar Jahren**: in a few years, **in wenigen Minuten**: in a few minutes, **mehr Rotwein**: more red wine, **mit Geld von ihrem Sparkonto**: with money from her savings account, **regelmäßig**: regularly, **schließlich**: eventually, **unsere berühmten Biere**: our famous beers, **unverheiratet**: unmarried, **über die schönen Weinberge am Kaiserstuhl**: about the beautiful Kaiserstuhl vineyards, **von Japan nach Deutschland**: to Germany from Japan, **Weinanbau**: viticulture, **weit weg**: far away, **weitere lokale Sehenswürdigkeiten**: other local sights

Short Story: "Kaiserstuhl Vineyards"

Naomi plant einen Urlaub. Sie lebt am Meer und möchte etwas anderes erleben.

Naomi is planning a vacation. She lives by the sea and prefers something different.

Naomi hat schon viel über die schönen Weinberge am Kaiserstuhl in Deutschland gehört. Es ist weit weg, also bucht Naomi einen Flug.

Naomi has heard a lot about the beautiful Kaiserstuhl vineyards in Germany. It is far away so Naomi books a flight.

Naomi ist unverheiratet und reist allein. Der Flug ist ein bisschen teuer. Aber sie kann sich das Ticket mit Geld von ihrem Sparkonto leisten.

Naomi is unmarried and traveling solo. The flight is a little bit expensive. But she can afford the ticket with money from her savings account.

Naomi besucht ihre Großeltern am Tag vor ihrer Abreise. Sie wünschen ihr alles Gute für die Reise. Oma möchte, dass Naomi die berühmten Rotweine probiert. Opa möchte, dass

Naomi viele Fotos macht.

Naomi visits her grandparents on the day before her departure. They wish her all the best for the trip. Grandma wants Naomi to try the famous red wines. Grandpa wants Naomi to take lots of photos.

Naomi fliegt jetzt hoch über den Wolken. Sie freut sich darauf, von Japan nach Deutschland zu reisen. Sie spricht nicht viel Deutsch, aber viele Deutsche sprechen gut Englisch. Naomi ist Japanerin und spricht auch fließend Englisch.

Naomi is now flying high above the clouds. She is excited to travel to Germany from Japan. She doesn't speak much German, but many Germans speak English well. Naomi is Japanese and also speaks English fluently.

Eine Durchsage ertönt: „Liebe Passagiere, wir landen in wenigen Minuten."

An announcement sounds, "Dear passengers, we will be landing in a few mintues."

Naomi ist voller Vorfreude. Sie landet in Zürich, Schweiz, eine Busstunde vom Kaiserstuhl entfernt. Sie kommt schließlich im Hotel an.

Naomi is filled with anticipation. She lands in Zurich, Switzerland, which is an hour away by bus from the Kaiserstuhl. She eventually arrives at the hotel.

Am nächsten Morgen besucht Naomi die berühmten Weinberge. Sie erkennt die grünen Hügel. Überall sieht sie bunte und duftende Weintrauben. Sie fühlt sich wie im Paradies.

The next morning, Naomi visits the famous vineyards. She recognizes the verdant hills. She sees colorful and fragrant wine grapes everywhere. She feels like she is in paradise.

Das ist jetzt Naomis neuer Lieblingsort in Deutschland. Sie macht Hunderte Fotos der Weinberge. Es besteht sogar die Möglichkeit, einige berühmte Rotweine zu probieren!

This is now Naomi's new favorite place in Germany. She takes hundreds of photos of the vineyards. There is even an opportunity to taste some famous red wines!

Es gibt Wanderwege in der Nähe. Naomi lernt viele Leute kennen. Mit einigen tauscht sie E-Mail-Adressen aus.

There are hiking trails nearby. Naomi meets many people. She exchanges email addresses with some.

Die Gerüchte sind wahr! Die meisten Deutschen können sehr gut Englisch sprechen. Einige Deutsche können sogar Japanisch!

The rumors are true! Most Germans can speak English very well. Some Germans can even speak Japanese!

Lena ist eine neue Freundin. Sie will Naomi weitere lokale Sehenswürdigkeiten zeigen. Sie besuchen ein Museum und Naomi lernt etwas über Weinanbau. Sie genießen gemeinsam ein entspanntes Mittagessen. Naomi kauft ein Dutzend Flaschen Kaiserstuhl-Rotweine und schenkt Lena eine Flasche.

Lena is a new friend. She wants to show Naomi other local sights. They visit a museum and Naomi learns about viticulture. They enjoy a relaxing lunch together. Naomi buys a dozen bottles of Kaiserstuhl red wines and gives a bottle to Lena as a gift.

„Wer kann schon einer weiteren Flasche Kaiserstuhler Rotwein widerstehen?", lacht Lena. „Mein Mann und ich trinken jeden Tag ein Glas Wein."

"Who can resist another bottle of Kaiserstuhl red wine?", laughs Lena. "My husband and I drink a glass of wine everyday!"

Naomi lächelt glücklich und sagt: „Ich werde vielleicht

nach Deutschland zurückkehren, nur um mehr Rotwein zu kaufen!"

Naomi smiles happily and says, "I might return to Germany just to buy more red wine!"

„Vergessen Sie nicht unsere berühmten Biere!", sagt Lena.

"Don't forget about our famous beers!", says Lena.

Naomi wacht an ihrem letzten Tag früh auf. Ihr Flug geht am frühen Nachmittag von Zürich aus. Lena und Naomi vereinbaren, regelmäßig in Kontakt zu bleiben. Naomi plant, in ein paar Jahren wieder nach Deutschland zu kommen. Das nächste Mal wird sie fließend Deutsch sprechen!

Naomi wakes up early on her last day. Her flight departs from Zurich in the early afternoon. Lena and Naomi agree to keep in touch regularly. Naomi plans to come back to Germany in a few years. Next time, she will be fluent in German!

Chapter 14

"Birthday in Baden-Baden" // "Geburtstag in Baden-Baden"

Photo of Baden-Baden by Roman Babakin.

Featured Vocabulary

bereit für unser Geburtstagfeier: ready for our birthday celebration, **Dackel**: Dachshund, **das Restaurant vor Ort**: the on-site restaurant, **die Gegenwart**: the present, **die Vergangenheit**: the past, **die Zukunft**: the future, **draußen oder drinnen**: outside or inside, **ein echtes Fabergé-Ei**: a real Fabergé egg, **ein spätes Mittagessen**: a late lunch, **eine Sammlung**: a collection, **eine Überraschung**: a surprise, **einen entspannenden Nachmittag**: a relaxing afternoon, **einen Thunfischsalat**: a tuna salad, **Florians Frau**: Florian's wife, **Florians Geburtstag**: Florian's birthday, **für deinen nächsten Geburtstag**: for your next birthday, **hat nichts vor**: has nothing planned, **Hühnchen mit Reis und Gemüse**: chicken with rice and vegetables, **nicht zu satt**: not too full, **sehr beeindruckt**: very impressed, **so eins**: one of these, **teuren Eiern aus Edelmetallen und Juwelen**: expensive eggs made of precious metals and jewels, **unglaublich teuer**: incredibly expensive, **über die Einladung**: about the invitation, **viele Baden-Badener**: many Baden-Baden residents, **Weltklasse-Käsespätzle und -Kirschenmichel**: world-class cheese noodles and cherry bread pudding, **zum Teilen**: to share

Short Story: "Birthday in Baden-Baden"

Heute ist Florians Geburtstag. Sein Sohn Johannes will mit ihm in Baden-Baden feiern. Er möchte mit ihm ins Fabergé-Museum und in die Caracalla-Thermen gehen.

Today is Florian's birthday. His son, Johannes, wants to celebrate with him in Baden-Baden. He'd like to go to the Fabergé Museum and the Caracalla thermal baths together.

Florian hat nichts vor und freut sich über die Einladung!

Florian has nothing planned and is happy about the invitation!

Sie kommen mit dem Auto zum Fabergé-Museum. Das Museum zeigt eine Sammlung von teuren Eiern aus Edelmetallen und Juwelen. Florian und Johannes sind beide sehr beeindruckt. Im Museum gibt es über siebenhundert solcher Fabergé-Eier.

They arrive by car to the Fabergé Museum. The museum features a collection of expensive eggs made of precious metals and jewels. Florian and Johannes are both very impressed. There are over seven hundred such Fabergé eggs in the museum.

„Ich würde mir gerne so eins kaufen", sagt Johannes.

"I'd love to buy one of these," says Johannes.

„Das wäre unglaublich teuer! Ein echtes Fabergé-Ei kostet Millionen," sagt Florian. „Die kommen aus Russland. Viele Baden-Badener kommen auch von dort."

"It would be incredibly expensive! A real Fabergé egg costs millions," says Florian. "They come from Russia. Many Baden-Baden residents also come from there."

Nach dem Museumsbesuch fahren Florian und Johannes zur Caracalla-Therme. Dort gibt es Innen- und Außenthermalbäder. Sie bieten auch Saunen und Massagen an. Die Leute kommen hierher, um sich zu verjüngen.

After the museum visit, Florian and Johannes drive to the Caracalla thermal baths. There are indoor and outdoor thermal baths there. They also offer saunas and massages. People come here to rejuvenate themselves.

„Willen Sie draußen oder drinnen baden?", fragt Johannes.

"Do you want to soak outside or inside?", asks Johannes.

„Die Luft ist draußen besser", antwortet Florian. „Ich möchte später auch eine Massage bekommen!"

"The air is better outside," replies Florian. "I'd like to get a massage later too!"

„Eine Massage wäre bestimmt toll,“ sagt Johannes. „Können wir später auch ein paar Minuten in der Sauna sitzen?“

"A massage would definitely be great," says Johannes. "Can we sit in the sauna for a few minutes later too?"

Die beiden genießen einen entspannenden Nachmittag in heißen und kalten Bädern, in der Sauna und zum Abschluss bei einer Massage.

They both enjoy a relaxing afternoon inside hot and cold baths, a sauna, and wrap up with a massage.

Jetzt sind sie hungrig. Sie gehen in das Restaurant vor Ort, um ein spätes Mittagessen einzunehmen. Florian bestellt Hühnchen mit Reis und Gemüse. Johannes bestellt einen Thunfischsalat und einen selbstgebackenen Kuchen zum Teilen.

Now they are hungry. They head to the on-site restaurant to take a late lunch. Florian orders chicken with rice and vegetables. Johannes orders a tuna salad and a homemade cake to share.

„Was für ein besonderer Tag heute!“, sagt Florian. „Wie schön, dass du so einen denkwürdigen Geburtstag geplant

hast. Ich werde auch für deinen nächsten Geburtstag eine Überraschung haben!"

"What a special day today!", says Florian. "You're so kind to plan such a memorable birthday. I will have a surprise for your next birthday too!"

Florian und Johannes fahren nach Hause und sprechen über die Vergangenheit, die Gegenwart und die Zukunft. Als sie zu Hause ankommen, werden sie von Florians Frau Carla und ihrem Dackel Milo freudig begrüßt.

Florian and Johannes drive home and talk about the past, present, and future. When they arrive home, they are happily greeted by Florian's wife, Carla, and their Dachshund, Milo.

„Willkommen zu Hause, meine Herren!", ruft Carla. „Hatten sie einen tollen Tag zusammen? Ich hoffe, sie sind nicht zu satt. Meine Weltklasse-Käsespätzle und -Kirschenmichel sind bereit für unser Geburtstagfeier heute Abend!"

"Welcome home, gentlemen!", exclaims Carla. "Did you have a great day together? I hope you're not too full. My world-class cheese noodles and cherry bread pudding are ready for our birthday celebration tonight!"

Chapter 15

"Freiburg Christmas Market" //
"Freiburger Weihnachtsmarkt"

Photo of German mulled wine by Alexander Raths.

Featured Vocabulary

bereit für Weihnachten: ready for Christmas, **bunte Lichter
und festliche Musik**: colorful lights and festive music, **dankbar**:
grateful, **die Feiertage**: the holidays, **die Prüfungen vorbei sind**:
the exams are over, **die Tür**: the door, **die Umzugskartons**: the
moving cardboard boxes, **die Vorbereitungen**: the preparations,
ein Schränkchen: a small cupboard, **eine kurze Pause**: a quick
break, **eine neue Wohnung**: a new apartment, **entfernt werden**:
be taken out, **fahren mit der Straßenbahn**: take the streetcar,
Flaschen mit Sprudelwasser: bottles of sparkling water, **fünf
Tassen**: five cups, **für ein Semester**: for one semester, **gebrannte
Mandeln**: roasted almonds, **Glühwein**: mulled wine, **Gudruns
beste Freunde**: Gudrun's best friends, **himmlische Gewürze**:
heavenly spices, **ihren eigenen Wegen**: their own paths, **ihrer
Grundschulzeit**: their elementary school days, **irgendwie Spaß**:
kind of fun, **klingt nach**: sounds like, **Landschaftsgemälde**:
landscape paintings, **mitmachen**: join in, **nach Berlin**: to Berlin,
sind geöffnet: are open, **Tüten mit Studentenfutter**: bags of
trail mix, **über das Wochenende**: over the weekend, **wie immer**:
as usual, **wundervolle Freunde**: wonderful friends, **zurzeit**:
currently, **zwei Wochen vor Weihnachten**: two weeks before
Christmas

Short Story: "Freiburg Christmas Market"

Es ist zwei Wochen vor Weihnachten. Gudrun zieht in eine neue Wohnung um.

It's two weeks before Christmas. Gudrun is moving into a new apartment.

Sie wohnt zurzeit in Freiburg und studiert Mathematik. Sie möchte gerne Mathelehrerin werden.

She currently lives in Freiburg and studies mathematics. She would like to become a math teacher.

Ihre Freunde kommen und helfen ihr über das Wochenende beim Umzug. Bastian, Tariq, Monika und Felix sind Gudruns beste Freunde. Sie kennen sich seit ihrer Grundschulzeit.

Her friends come and help her move over the weekend. Bastian, Tariq, Monika, and Felix are Gudrun's best friends. They have known each other since their elementary school days.

Sie beginnen den Umzug um 9 Uhr morgens nach dem gemeinsamen Frühstück.

They start the move at 9 a.m. after eating breakfast together.

Bastian trägt ein Schränkchen. „Kannst du bitte die Tür öffnen?", fragt er Gudrun.

Bastian is carrying a small cupboard. "Can you please open the door?", he asks Gudrun.

Gudrun hilft ihm mit der Tür und sagt: „Danke für deine Hilfe!"

Gudrun helps him with the door and says, "Thanks for your help!"

Tariq ordnet und verschließt die Umzugskartons. „Das macht irgendwie Spaß!", sagt er.

Tariq is organizing and sealing the moving cardboard boxes. "This is kind of fun!", he says.

„Sollen der Herd und der Kühlschrank auch entfernt werden? Und was ist mit dem Landschaftsgemälde?", fragt Felix.

"Should the stove and refrigerator be taken out too? And what about the landscape paintings?", asks Felix.

„Ich habe hier Flaschen mit Sprudelwasser und Tüten mit Studentenfutter. Wo soll ich sie hinstellen?", fragt Monika.

"I have bottles of sparkling water and bags of trail mix here. Where should I put them?", asks Monika.

„Wohin ziehst du?", will Felix wissen. Er macht eine kurze

Pause.

"Where are you moving to?", Felix wants to know. He is taking a quick break.

„Nach Berlin. Aber ich bin nur für ein Semester dort. Dann komme ich zurück nach Freiburg," antwortet Gudrun.

"To Berlin. But I'm only there for one semester. Then I'll come back to Freiburg," replies Gudrun.

„Berlin klingt nach viel Spaß", sagt Felix. „Wir werden dich hier ein ganzes Semester lang vermissen!"

"Berlin sounds like a lot of fun," says Felix. "We'll miss you here for a whole semester!"

Sie beenden die Vorbereitungen für den Umzug. Es ist fast Abend. Der Weihnachtsmarkt in Freiburg öffnet bald. Es schneit sogar ein bisschen.

They finish the preparations for the move. It's almost evening. The Christmas market in Freiburg opens soon. It's even snowing a little bit.

Gudrun und ihre Freunde fahren mit der Straßenbahn zum Weihnachtsmarkt. Überall gibt es bunte Lichter und festliche Musik. Die Stände sind geöffnet und bieten Glühwein,

gebrannte Mandeln, Crêpes und vieles mehr an.

Gudrun and her friends take the streetcar to the Christmas market. There are colorful lights and festive music everywhere. The stands are open and offering mulled wine, roasted almonds, crêpes, and much more.

Bastian freut sich. „Ich will einen Glühwein! Wer will mitmachen?"

Bastian is delighted. "I want a mulled wine! Who wants to join in?"

Alle wollen mitmachen. Die Verkäuferin gibt ihnen fünf Tassen. Der Glühwein schmeckt wie himmlische Gewürze in der Winterkälte.

Everyone wants to join in. The seller gives them five cups. The mulled wine tastes like heavenly spices in the winter cold.

„Ich bin froh, dass die Prüfungen vorbei sind," sagt Tariq. „Jetzt können wir die Feiertage wirklich genießen."

"I'm glad the exams are over," says Tariq. "Now, we can truly enjoy the holidays."

Die fünf Freunde reden, lachen und erkunden den Weihnachtsmarkt, bis er schließt.

The five friends talk, laugh, and explore the Christmas market until it closes.

Sie alle gehen auf ihren eigenen Wegen nach Hause. Gudrun ist dankbar, so wundervolle Freunde zu haben. Und alle fünf werden, wie immer, alles füreinander tun, was sie können.

They all go home by their own paths. Gudrun is grateful to have such wonderful friends. And all five of them will do everything they can for one another, as usual.

Gudrun ist bereit für Weihnachten und den Umzug nach Berlin!

Gudrun is ready for Christmas and the move to Berlin!

Chapter 16

"Westweg Journey" // "Westweg Reise"

Hiking signs in the Black Forest by Edith Czech.

Featured Vocabulary

am zweiten Tag: on the second day, **an einem Samstag**: on a Saturday, **bei der Polizei**: with the police, **bei der Post**: at the post office, **die frohe Botschaft**: the good news, **die Zeitung**: the newspaper, **durch ganz Deutschland**: throughout Germany, **eigentlich**: actually, **ein gutes Einkommen**: a good income, **ein paar Fotos**: some photos, **eine meiner längsten Wanderungen**: one of my longest hikes, **eine Wanderroute**: a hiking path, **einen interessanten Artikel**: an interesting article, **einen längeren Urlaub**: a longer vacation, **fit genug**: fit enough, **genau eine Woche später**: exactly one week later, **gesund bleiben**: stay healthy, **glücklicherweise**: fortunately, **ihre Ärztin**: her (female) doctor, **im Wald**: in the forest, **immer**: always, **in der Nähe des Startpunkts**: near the starting point, **in einem Lebensmittelladen**: at a grocery store, **Kaffee und Kuchen**: coffee and cake, **kann nicht widersprechen**: can't argue, **keine Zweifel**: no doubts, **körperlichen Fähigkeiten**: physical abilities, **nicht viel Urlaub**: not much vacation, **seit zwölf Jahren**: for twelve years, **sicherlich**: certainly, **sie unterhalten sich**: they converse, **Sieglindes Leidenschaft**: Sieglinde's passion, **Telefonnummern**: phone numbers, **unterwegs**: along the way, **über eine Woche**: over a week, **viele Tipps**: many tips, **von der**

Arbeit: from work, **zu überleben**: to survive, **zufrieden**: satisfied

Short Story: "Westweg Journey"

Angela liest die Zeitung. Sie sieht einen interessanten Artikel über den Westweg. Das ist eine Wanderroute, für die man über eine Woche braucht. Angela zeigt ihrem Mann den Artikel.

Angela is reading the newspaper. She sees an interesting article about the Westweg. It's a hiking route that takes over a week to complete. Angela shows her husband the article.

„Ich will das machen!", sagt sie zu ihm.

"I want to do this!", she says to him.

Rolf kann nicht widersprechen. Angela macht alles, was sie sich vornimmt. Sie sind seit zwölf Jahren veheiratet und er unterstützt sie immer.

Rolf can't argue. Angela does everything she puts her mind to. They've been married for twelve years and he always supports her.

Rolf arbeitet bei der Polizei und hat ein gutes Einkommen. Aber er kann nicht viel Urlaub von der Arbeit nehmen.

Angela arbeitet bei der Post und kann einen längeren Urlaub nehmen.

Rolf works with the police and has a good income. But he can't take much vacation from work. Angela works at the post office and can take a longer vacation.

„Ich bin erstaunt, dass du so gut drauf bist", sagt Rolf zu seiner Frau.

"I'm amazed you're in such a fantastic mood," Rolf tells his wife.

„Kannst du dir vorstellen, dass ich bald den Westweg wandern werde?", fragt Angela.

"Can you believe that I'll be hiking the Westweg soon?", asks Angela.

„Na ja, eigentlich...", stammelt Rolf.

"Well, actually...", stammers Rolf.

„Es ist sicherlich eine meiner längsten Wanderungen!", ruft Angela.

"It's certainly one of my longest hikes!", exclaims Angela.

Angela ruft ihre Ärztin an. Sie möchte wissen, ob sie fit genug für die Wanderung ist. Glücklicherweise hat die Ärztin keine

Zweifel an Angelas körperlichen Fähigkeiten. Sie gibt Angela viele Tipps, wie sie auf einer so langen Wanderung gesund bleiben kann.

Angela calls her doctor. She wants to know if she is fit enough for the hike. Fortunately, the doctor has no doubts about Angela's physical abilities. She shares many tips with Angela on how to stay healthy on such a long hike.

Sie beginnt ihre Wanderung an einem Samstag. Unterwegs kauft sie in einem Lebensmittelladen Brot, Obst, Snacks und Wasser. Sie kauft genug ein, um über eine Woche zu überleben.

She starts her hike on a Saturday. Along the way, she buys bread, fruit, snacks, and water at a grocery store. She buys enough to survive for over a week.

Sie parkt ihr Auto in der Nähe des Startpunkts des Westwegs. Die Wanderung beginnt endlich! Angela ist aufgeregt und macht fröhlich ein paar Fotos von den schönen Landschaften um sie herum.

She parks her car near the starting point of the Westweg trail. The hike is finally beginning! Angela is excited and happily takes some photos of the beautiful landscapes around her.

Am zweiten Tag der Wanderung trifft Angela auf Sieglinde. Sie wandert auch allein auf dem Westweg. Sie unterhalten sich und werden schnell Freunde. Sie sitzen zusammen auf einer Bank im Wald.

On the second day of the hike, Angela meets Sieglinde. She is also hiking the Westweg alone. They converse and quickly become friends. They sit together on a bench in the forest.

Sieglinde ist durch ganz Deutschland gewandert. Angela ist begeistert von Sieglindes Leidenschaft fürs Wandern.

Sieglinde has hiked throughout Germany. Angela is inspired by Sieglinde's passion for hiking.

Genau eine Woche später ist die Wanderung zu Ende! Es war nicht leicht, aber jetzt sind sie zufrieden. Sieglinde lädt Angela in der nächsten Woche zu Kaffee und Kuchen ein. Angela nimmt gerne an. Sie tauschen Telefonnummern aus, um in Kontakt zu bleiben.

Exactly one week later, the hike is over. It wasn't easy, but now they are satisfied. Sieglinde invites Angela for coffee and cake sometime next week. Angela gladly accepts. They exchange phone numbers to stay in touch.

Als Angela nach Hause kommt, teilt sie Rolf die frohe

Botschaft mit. Sie essen in ihrem Lieblingsrestaurant zu Abend. Rolf ist glücklich, Angela wiederzusehen.

When Angela arrives home, she shares the happy news with Rolf. They eat dinner at their favorite restaurant. Rolf is happy to see Angela again.

In ein paar Tagen wird Angela wieder zur Arbeit gehen. Dann kann sie ihren nächsten Urlaub planen!

In a few more days, Angela will go back to work. Then she can start planning her next vacation!

German A1 Vocabulary Glossary // Deutsch A1 Vokabelglossar

A

ab: from

aber: but, however

abfahren: (to) depart, (to) leave, (to) drive off

(die) Abfahrt: (the) departure, (the) descent

abgeben: (to) deliver, (to) submit, (to) give

abholen: (to) pick up, (to) collect

(der) Absender: (the) sender

Achtung: attention, caution, warning

(die) Adresse: (the) address

alle, alles: all, everything

allein: alone, only

also: so, thus, therefore

alt: old, aged

(das) Alter: (the) age

an: on, to, at

anbieten: (to) offer, (to) provide

(das) Angebot: (the) offer

andere: other, others

anfangen: (to) start, (to) begin

(der) Anfangen: (the) beginning, (the) start

anklicken: (to) click on

ankommen: (to) arrive

(die) Ankunft: (the) arrival

ankreuzen: (to) check off, (to) tick off

anmachen: (to) turn on, (to) put on

(sich) anmelden: (to) log in, (to) register

(die) Anmeldung: (the) registration, (the) application

(die) Anrede: (the) salutation, (the) form of address, (the) title

anrufen: (to) call

(der) Anruf: (the) call, (the) phone call

(die) Ansage: (the) announcement

(der) Anschluss: (the) connection

antworten: (to) answer, (to) reply

(die) Antwort: (the) answer

(die) Anzeige: (the) display, (the) advertisement

(sich) anziehen: (to) get dressed, (to) put on clothes

(das) Apartment: (the) apartment

(der) Apfel: (the) apple

(der) Appetit: (the) appetite

arbeiten: (to) work

(die) Arbeit: (the) work

arbeitslos: unemployed

(der) Arbeitsplatz: (the) workplace

(der) Arm: (the) arm

(der) Arzt: (the) doctor

auch: also, even, too

auf: on, to, at, up

(die) Aufgabe: (the) task

aufhören: (to) stop, (to) quit

aufstehen: (to) stand up, (to) get up

(der) Aufzug: (the) elevator

(das) Auge: (the) eye

aus: from, off, out

(der) Ausflug: (the) excursion, (the) trip

ausfüllen: (to) fill in, (to) fill out

(der) Ausgang: (the) exit, (the) output

(die) Auskunft: (the) information

(das) Ausland: (the) foreign country

(der) Ausländer: (the) foreigner

ausländisch: foreign

ausmachen: (to) constitute, (to) identify

(die) Aussage: (the) statement

aussehen: (to) look, (to) appear

aussteigen: (to) get out, (to) get off, (to) exit

(der) Ausweis: (the) identification card

(sich) ausziehen: (to) undress, (to) take off one's clothes

(das) Auto: (the) car

(die) Autobahn: (the) highway, (the) freeway

(der) Automat: (the) vending machine

automatisch: automatic, automatically

B

(das) Baby: (the) baby

(die) Bäckerei: (the) bakery

(das) Bad: (the) bathroom, (the) bath

baden: (to) bathe

(die) Bahn: (the) railroad, (the) train

(der) Bahnhof: (the) train station

(der) Bahnsteig: (the) train platform

bald: soon

(der) Balkon: (the) balcony

(die) Banane: (the) banana

(die) Bank: (the) bank

bar: cash

(der) Bauch: (the) stomach, (the) belly

(der) Baum: (the) tree

(der) Beamte: (the) civil servant, (the) official

bedeuten: (to) signify, (to) mean

beginnen: (to) begin, (to) start

bei: with, at, for

beide: both

(das) Bein: (the) leg

(das) Beispiel: (the) example

bekannt: known, well-known

(der) Bekannte: (the) friend, (the) acquaintance

bekommen: (to) get, (to) obtain, (to) receive

benutzen: (to) utilize, (to) use

(der) Beruf: (the) occupation, (the) profession

besetzt: occupied, staffed, manned

besichtigen: (to) visit, (to) view, (to) inspect

besser: better, superior, improved

(am) besten: best, ideally

bestellen: (to) order

besuchen: (to) visit, (to) attend

(das) Bett: (the) bed

bezahlen: (to) pay, (to) pay for

(das) Bier: (the) beer

(das) Bild: (the) picture, (the) image

billig: cheap, inexpensive

(die) Birne: (the) pear

bis: until, to, up to

bisschen: little, a bit

bitte: please

(die) Bitte: (the) request

bitten: (to) ask for, (to) request

bitter: bitter, acerbic

bleiben: (to) stay, (to) remain

(der) Bleistift: (the) pencil

(der) Blick: (the) view, (the) look

(die) Blume: (the) flower

(der) Bogen: (the) bow, (the) arch

böse: evil, bad, nasty, wicked

brauchen: (to) need, (to) require

breit: wide, broad

(der) Brief: (the) letter

(die) Briefmarke: (the) postage stamp

bringen: (to) bring

(das) Brot: (the) bread

(das) Brötchen: (the) bread roll, (the) bun

(der) Bruder: (the) brother

(das) Buch: (the) book

(der) Buchstabe: (the) alphabet letter

buchstabieren: (to) spell, (to) spell out

(der) Bus: (the) bus

(die) Butter: (the) butter

C

(das) Café: (the) café

(die) CD: (the) CD

(der) Chef: (the) boss

circa/ca.: approximately

(der) Computer: (the) computer

D

da: there, since, as, because

(die) Dame: (the) lady

daneben: next to it, beside it

danken: (to) thank

(der) Dank: (the) thanks

danke: thank you, thanks

dann: then, than

(das) Datum: (the) date

dauern: (to) last for

dein: yours, your

denn: because, for

der, die, das: the (masculine, feminine, neutral)

dich: you, yourself, thee

diese: this, these

dir: to you, for you

(der) Doktor: (the) doctor

(das) Doppelzimmer: (the) double room

(das) Dorf: (the) village

dort: there, over there

dorther: from there

dorthin: to there

draußen: outside, outdoors

drucken: (to) print

(der) Drucker: (the) printer

drücken: (to) squeeze, (to) press

durch: through, by

(die) Durchsage: (the) announcement

dürfen: may, (to be) allowed

(der) Durst: (the) thirst

(sich) duschen: (to) take a shower

(die) Dusche: (the) shower

E

(die) Ecke: (the) corner

(die) Ehefrau: (the) wife

(die) Ehemann: (the) husband, (the) spouse

(das) Ei: (the) egg

eilig: hurried, hasty

ein, eine: a, an, one (masculine/neutral, feminine)

einfach: simple, easy

(der) Eingang: (the) entrance

einkaufen: (to) shop

einladen: (to) invite

(die) Einladung: (the) invitation

einmal: once

einsteigen: (to) get on board, (to) get in, (to) enter

(der) Eintritt: (the) entry, (the) admission

(das) Einzelzimmer: (the) single room

(die) Eltern: (the) parents

(die) E-Mail: (the) email

(der) Empfänger: (the) recipient, (the) receiver

empfehlen: (to) recommend, (to) suggest

enden: (to) finish, (to) end

(das) Ende: (the) end

entschuldigen: (to) apologize, (to) excuse

(die) Entschuldigung: (the) apology

er: he

(das) Ergebnis: (the) result

erklären: (to) explain, (to) declare

erlauben: (to) allow, (to) permit

(der) Erwachsene: (the) adult

erzählen: (to) tell

es: it

essen: (to) eat

(das) Essen: (the) food, (the) meal

euer: your (plural)

F

fahren: (to) drive, (to) ride, (to) travel

(der) Fahrer: (the) driver

(die) Fahrkarte: (the) ride ticket

(das) Fahrrad: (the) bicycle

falsch: wrong, false, incorrect

(die) Familie: (the) family

(der) Familienname: (the) surname, (the) family name

(der) Familienstand: (the) marital status

(die) Farbe: (the) color

(das) Fax: (the) fax

(der) Feiertag: (the) public holiday

feiern: (to) celebrate, (to) party

fehlen: (to) be missing, (to) be absent

(der) Fehlen: (the) error, (the) mistake

fernsehen: (to) watch television

fertig: finished, ready

(das) Feuer: (the) fire

(das) Fieber: (the) fever

(der) Film: (the) movie

finden: (to) find

(die) Firma: (the) company

(der) Fisch: (the) fish

(die) Flasche: (the) bottle

(das) Fleisch: (the) meat, (the) flesh

fliegen: (to) fly

(der) Flughafen: (the) airport

(das) Flugzeug: (the) airplane

(das) Formular: (the) form

(das) Foto: (the) photo

fragen: (to) ask

(die) Frage: (the) question

(die) Frau: (the) woman, (the) wife

frei: free, complimentary

(die) Freizeit: (the) leisure time

fremd: foreign, strange

(sich) freuen: (to) be happy, (to) be pleased

(der) Freund: (the) friend

früher: earlier, before, in the past

frühstücken: (to) have breakfast

(das) Frühstück: (the) breakfast

(die) Führung: (the) management, (the) guidance, (the) leadership

für: for

(der) Fuß: (the) foot

(der) Fußball: (the) soccer, (the) soccer ball

G

(der) Garten: (the) garden

(der) Gast: (the) guest

geben: (to) give, (to) provide

geboren: (to) be born

(das) Geburtsjahr: (the) birth year

(der) Geburtort: (the) birthplace

(der) Geburtstag: (the) birthday

gefallen: (to) be pleased, (to) like

gegen: versus, against

gehen: (to) go, (to) walk

gehören: (to) belong to, (to) include

(das) Geld: (the) money

(das) Gemüse: (the) vegetable(s)

(das) Gepäck: (the) luggage, (the) baggage

gerade: straight, just, even

geradeaus: straight ahead

gern(e): with pleasure, gladly

(das) Geschäft: (the) business, (the) store

(das) Geschenk: (the) gift, (the) present

(die) Geschwister: (the) siblings

(das) Gespräch: (the) conversation, (the) interview

gestern: yesterday

gestorben: (to) have died, (to) be deceased

(das) Getränk: (the) drink, (the) beverage

(das) Gewicht: (the) weight

gewinnen: (to) win, (to) gain

(das) Glas: (the) glass

glauben: (to) believe

gleich: equivalent

(das) Gleis: (the) track, (the) rail

(das) Glück: (the) happiness, (the) luck

glücklich: happy, happily, lucky

(der) Glückwunsch: (the) congratulations

gratulieren: (to) congratulate

grillen: (to) barbecue, (to) grill

groß: large, big, great, tall, grand

(die) Größe: (the) size

(die) Großeltern: (the) grandparents

(die) Großmutter: (the) grandmother

(der) Großvater: (the) grandfather

(die) Gruppe: (the) group

(der) Gruß: (the) greeting

gültig: valid, applicable, effective

günstig: cheap, convenient, favorable

gut: good, well

H

(das) Haar: (the) hair

haben: (to) have

(das) Hähnchen: (the) chicken

(die) Halbpension: (the) half-board accommodation

(die) Halle: (the) hall

hallo: hello, hi

halten: (to) hold, (to) keep

(die) Haltestelle: (the) stop, (the) bus stop

(die) Hand: (the) hand

(das) Handy: (the) cell phone

(das) Haus: (the) house

(die) Hausaufgabe: (the) homework

(die) Hausfrau: (the) housewife

(der) Hausmann: (the) houseman

(die) Heimat: (the) homeland, (the) home country

heiraten: (to) marry

heißen: (to) be called

helfen: (to) help, (to) assist

hell: bright, light

(der) Herd: (the) stove

(der) Herr: (the) Lord, (the) gentleman

herzlich: cordial, hearty, warm

heute: today, nowadays

hier: here

(die) Hilfe: (the) help, (the) aid, (the) assistance

hinten: at the back

(das) Hobby: (the) hobby

hoch: high, highly

(die) Hochzeit: (the) wedding

holen: (to) get, (to) fetch, (to) pick up

hören: (to) listen, (to) hear

(das) Hotel: (the) hotel

(der) Hund: (the) dog

(der) Hunger: (the) hunger

I

ich: I

ihm: to/from him, to/from it

ihn: him

ihr: you (plural), to/from her

immer: always, ever, all the time

in: in, into, at

(die) Information: (the) information

international: international, internationally

(das) Internet: (the) Internet

J

ja: yes, yeah

(die) Jacke: (the) jacket

jeder, jede, jedes: each, every (masculine, feminine, neutral)

jetzt: now

(der) Job: (the) job

(der) Jugendliche: (the) young person, (the) teenager

jung: young, youthful

(der) Junge: (the) boy

K

(der) Kaffee: (the) coffee

kaputt: broken

(die) Karte: (the) map, (the) card

(die) Kreditkarte: (the) credit card

(die) Kartoffel: (the) potato

(die) Kasse: (the) cash register

kaufen: (to) buy, (to) purchase

kein: none, not any of

kennen: (to) know, (to) be familiar with

kennenlernen: (to) get to know someone

(das) Kind: (the) child

(der) Kindergarten: (the) kindergarten, (the) nursery school

(das) Kino: (the) movie theater, (the) cinema

klar: clear, clearly

(die) Klasse: (the) class

(die) Kleidung: (the) clothes, (the) clothing

klein: small, little, short, modest, dinky

kochen: (to) cook

(der) Koffer: (the) suitcase

(der) Kollege: (the) colleague

kommen: (to) come

können: can, (to) be able to

(das) Konto: (the) account

(der) Kopf: (the) head

kosten: (to) cost

krank: sick, ill

kriegen: (to) get, (to) obtain

(die) Küche: (the) kitchen

(der) Kuchen: (the) cake

(der) Kugelschreiber: (the) ballpoint pen

(der) Kühlschrank: (the) refrigerator

kulturell: cultural, culturally

(sich) kümmern: (to) take care of

(der) Kunde: (the) customer, (the) client

(der) Kurs: (the) course

kurz: short, brief, briefly

L

lachen: (to) laugh

(der) Laden: (the) store

lang: long (distance), lengthy

lange: long (time), lengthy

langsam: slow, slowly

laufen: (to) run, (to) walk

laut: loud, according to

leben: (to) live

(das) Leben: (the) life

(die) Lebensmittel: (the) foodstuffs

ledig: single, unmarried

legen: (to) lay, (to) place, (to) put

(der) Lehrer: (the) teacher

leicht: easy, light, lightweight

leider: unfortunate, unfortunately

leise: quiet, quietly

lernen: (to) learn

lesen: (to) read

letzte: last, final

(die) Leute: (the) people

(das) Licht: (the) light

liebe: dear (female)

lieber: dear (male), rather, preferably

(das) Lied: (the) song

liegen: (to) lie (placement), (to) be located

links: left, to the left

(der) Lkw: (the) truck

(das) Lokal: (the) restaurant, (the) eatery, (the) pub

(die) Lösung: (the) solution

lustig: funny, amusing

M

machen: (to) make, (to) do

(das) Mädchen: (the) girl

man: one, you

(der) Mann: (the) man

männlich: male, masculine

(die) Maschine: (the) machine

(das) Meer: (the) sea

mehr: more

mein: my, mine

(die) meisten: (the) most

(der) Mensch: (the) human being

mieten: (to) rent, (to) hire

(die) Miete: (the) rent

(die) Milch: (the) milk

mit: with

mitbringen: (to) bring along

mitkommen: (to) come along

mitmachen: (to) join in, (to) participate

mitnehmen: (to) take along

(die) Mitte: (the) center, (the) middle

(die) Möbel: (the) furniture

möchten: would like to

mögen: (to) like

möglich: possible

(der) Moment: (the) moment

morgen: tomorrow, morning

müde: tired, weary

(der) Mund: (the) mouth

müssen: must

(die) Mutter: (the) mother

N

nach: to, after, according to, by

nächste: next

(der) Name: (the) name

nehmen: (to) take, (to) use

nein: no

neu: new

nicht: not

nichts: nothing

nie: never

noch: still, yet

normal: normal, standard, ordinary

(die) Nummer: (the) number

nur: only, just

O

oben: above, at the top, upstairs, overhead

(das) Obst: (the) fruit

oder: or

öffnen: (to) open, (to) unlock

oft: often, frequently

ohne: without

(das) Öl: (the) oil

(die) Oma: (the) grandma

(der) Opa: (the) grandpa

(die) Ordnung: (the) order, (the) tidiness

(der) Ort: (the) place

P

(das) Papier: (the) paper

(der) Partner: (the) partner

(die) Party: (the) party, (the) celebration

(der) Pass: (the) passport

(die) Pause: (the) break

(der) Plan: (the) plan

(der) Platz: (the) place, (the) spot, (the) square

(die) Polizei: (the) police

(die) Pommes frites: (the) French fries

(die) Post: (the) post office

(die) Postleitzahl: (the) zip code, (the) postal code

(das) Praktikum: (the) internship

(die) Praxis: (the) practice, (the) practical experience

(der) Preis: (the) price

(das) Problem: (the) problem

(der) Prospekt: (the) brochure

(die) Prüfung: (the) exam, (the) audit

pünktlich: punctual, on time

R

Rad fahren: (to) ride a bike

rauchen: (to) smoke

(der) Raum: (the) room, (the) space

(die) Rechnung: (the) bill, (the) invoice

rechts: right, to the right

(der) Regen: (the) rain

regnen: (to) rain

(der) Reis: (the) rice

(die) Reise: (the) journey, (the) trip

reisen: (to) travel

(die) Reparatur: (the) repair

reparieren: (to) repair

(das) Restaurant: (the) restaurant

(die) Rezeption: (the) reception, (the) reception desk

richtig: right, correct

riechen: (to) smell, (to) sniff

ruhig: quiet, calm

S

(der) Saft: (the) juice

sagen: (to) say, (to) tell, (to) speak

(der) Salat: (the) salad

(das) Salz: (the) salt

(der) Satz: (the) sentence, (the) phrase

(die) S-Bahn: (the) suburban train

(der) Schalter: (the) switch

scheinen: (to) seem, (to) appear

schicken: (to) send

(das) Schild: (the) sign, (the) shield

(der) Schinken: (the) ham

schlafen: (to) sleep

schlecht: bad, poorly

schließen: (to) close, (to) conclude, (to) shut

(der) Schluss: (the) conclusion, (the) end

(der) Schlüssel: (the) key

schmecken: (to) taste

schnell: fast, quick

schon: already, really, all right

schön: nice, beautiful, great

(der) Schrank: (the) cupboard, (the) cabinet, (the) wardrobe

schreiben: (to) write

(der) Schuh: (the) shoe

(die) Schule: (the) school

(der) Schüler: (the) student

schwer: heavy, difficult

(die) Schwester: (the) sister

(das) Schwimmbad: (the) swimming pool

schwimmen: (to) swim

(der) See: (the) lake

sehen: (to) see, (to) view

(die) Sehenswürdigkeit: (the) sight, (the) place of interest

sehr: very

sein: (to) be

seit: since

selbstständig: independent, self-employed

sie: she, they, her, them

Sie: you (formal)

so: so, such, thus

(das) Sofa: (the) sofa

sofort: immediately, at once

(der) Sohn: (the) son

sollen: should

(die) Sonne: (the) sun

spät: late, tardy

später: later, subsequent

(die) Speisekarte: (the) menu

spielen: (to) play

(der) Sport: (the) sport

(die) Sprache: (the) language

sprechen: (to) speak, (to) talk

(die) Stadt: (the) city, (the) town

stehen: (to) stand, (to) be upstanding

(die) Stelle: (the) job, (the) position

stellen: (to) place, (to) set, (to) arrange

(der) Stock: (the) stick, (the) cane

(die) Straße: (the) street, (the) road

(die) Straßenbahn: (the) tram, (the) streetcar

studieren: (to) study

(der) Student: (the) student

(das) Studium: (the) study program

(die) Stunde: (the) hour

suchen: (to) seek, (to) look for

T

tanzen: (to) dance

(die) Tasche: (the) bag, (the) pocket

(das) Taxi: (the) cab

(der) Tee: (the) tea

(der) Teil: (the) part (of)

(das) Telefon: (the) phone

telefonieren: (to) make a phone call

(der) Termin: (the) appointment

(der) Test: (the) test

teuer: expensive, costly

(der) Text: (the) text (words), (the) textbook

(das) Thema: (the) topic

(das) Ticket: (the) ticket

(der) Tisch: (the) table

(die) Tochter: (the) daughter

(die) Toilette: (the) toilet, (the) restroom

(die) Tomate: (the) tomato

tot: dead, lifeless, extinct

(sich) treffen: (to) meet up

(die) Treppe: (the) stairs, (the) staircase

trinken: (to) drink

tschüss: bye

tun: (to) do

U

über: over, about, via

übernachten: (to) stay overnight

überweisen: (to) transfer, (to) remit

(die) Uhr: (the) clock, (the) watch

um: around, at, about

umziehen: (to) move, (to) relocate

und: and

unser, unsere: our (masculine/neutral, feminine)

unten: below, underneath, downstairs

unter: under, among

(der) Unterricht: (the) lesson

unterschreiben: (to) sign, (to) subscribe, (to) endorse

(die) Unterschrift: (the) signature

(der) Urlaub: (the) vacation

V

(der) Vater: (the) father

verboten: prohibited, banned

verdienen: (to) earn, (to) make

(der) Verein: (the) union, (the) club

verheiratet: married

verkaufen: (to) sell

(der) Verkäufer: (the) seller, (the) vendor

vermieten: (to) rent out, (to) let

(der) Vermieter: (the) landlord, (the) lessor

verstehen: (to) understand

(der) Verwandte: (the) relative

viel: much, a lot

vielleicht: maybe, perhaps

von: from, of, by

vor: before, in front of

(der) Vorname: (the) first name, (the) given name

(die) Vorsicht: (the) caution

(sich) vorstellen: (to) introduce oneself

(die) Vorwahl: (the) area code (phone dialing)

W

wandern: (to) hike

wann: when

warten: (to) wait

warum: why

was: what

was für ein: what kind of

(sich) waschen: (to) wash oneself

(das) Wasser: (the) water

weiblich: female, feminine

(der) Wein: (the) wine

weit: far, wide

weiter: further, additional

welcher, welche, welches: which (masculine, feminine, neutral)

(die) Welt: (the) world

wenig: few, a little

wer: who

werden: (to) become

(das) Wetter: (the) weather

wichtig: important

wie: how, as, like

wiederholen: (to) repeat

(das) Wiederhören: (the) goodbye, (the) until next time (when not face-to-face)

(das) Wiedersehen: (the) goodbye, (the) until next time (when meeting in-person)

wie viel: how much

willkommen: (to) welcome

(der) Wind: (the) wind

wir: we

wissen: (to) know (facts)

wo: where

woher: where from

wohin: where to

wohnen: (to) reside

(die) Wohnung: (the) apartment

wollen: (to) want

(das) Wort: (the) word

wunderbar: wonderful, delightful

Z

zahlen: (to) pay

(die) Zeit: (the) time

zurzeit: currently, at present

(die) Zeitung: (the) newspaper

(die) Zigarette: (the) cigarette

(das) Zimmer: (the) room

(der) Zoll: (the) customs

zu: to, too, at

zufrieden: satisfied, contented

(der) Zug: (the) train

zurück: back, behind, backwards

zusammen: together

zwischen: between

We'd Love to Hear Your Thoughts!

We hope you've enjoyed reading this book and find it to be a valuable addition to your collection of German language learning resources. It would brighten our day if you took a minute to leave a review of your thoughts on this book's Amazon page via the **QR code** or this **URL web link:**

https://www.amazon.com/review/create-review?asin=B0D9MXP8RP. **Danke schön und alles Gute! (Thank you and all the best!)**

Resources

1. A1_SD1_Wortliste_02. Goethe Institut, https://www.goethe.de/pro/relaunch/prf/de/A1_SD1_Wortliste_02.pdf. Accessed 30 Mar. 2024.

2. Babakin, Roman. "Panaromic view on Baden-Baden church and the city." Depositphotos, depositphotos.com/photo/panoramic-view-on-baden-baden-church-and-the-city-105817592.html.

3. Czech, Edith. "Hiking signs in the Black Forest." Depositphotos, depositphotos.com/photo/hiking-signs-in-the-black-forest-45265317.html.

4. Dzinnik, Darius. "Asparagus with black forest ham, carrots and hollandaise sauce." Depositphotos, depositphotos.com/photo/asparagus-black-forest-ham-carrots-hollandaise-sauce-471214008.html.

5. Eckert, Peter. "Idyllic place in Kaiserstuhl wine region,Black Forest, Germany." Depositphotos, depositphotos.com/photo/idyllic-place-kaiserstuhl-wine-region-black-forest-germany-418284452.html.

6. Erb, Johannes. "White winter mountain landscape. Snow in the Black Forest. View from a mountain peak, Feldberg, Germany." Depositphotos, depositphotos.com/photo/white-winter-mountain-landscape-snow-black-forest-view-mountain-peak-404165966.html.

7. "Fabergé Museum | Baden-Baden EN." Baden-Baden EN, www.baden-baden.com/en/media/attractions/faberge-museum#.

8. Fischbach, Frank. "Gertelsbacher Waterfalls in autumn, Black Forest, Germany." Depositphotos, depositphotos.com/photo/gertelsbacher-waterfalls-in-autumn-black-forest-germany-14571155.html.

9. Gajic, Vladislav. "Roller coaster in Europapark, Rust, Germany." Depositphotos, depositphotos.com/photo/roller-coaster-europapark-rust-germany-368055014.html.

10. Gourlay, Sharon. "Hohenbaden Castle: Everything You Need to Know Before You Go - Germany Footsteps." Germany Footsteps, 15 Apr. 2024, germanyfootsteps.com/hohenbaden-castle-baden-baden.

11. Iastremskiy, Leonid. "Plate with piece of tasty cherry cake on pink background." Depositphotos, depositphotos.com/photo/plate-piece-tasty-cherry-cake-pink-background-664672870.html.

12. Kinchokawat, Amnach. "Lake Titisee Neustadt in the Black Forest." Depositphotos, depositphotos.com/photo/lake-titisee-neustadt-in-the-black-forest-186921656.html.

13. Klootwijk, Michiel. "TRIBERG, GERMANY - AUGUST 21 2017: Biggest Cuckoo Clock in the W." Depositphotos, depositphotos.com/photo/triberg-germany-august-21-2017-biggest-cuckoo-clock-in-the-w-167316276.html.

14. Kotikova, Kateryna. Rural landscape. Vineyard and grapes bunches. depositphotos.com/vector/rural-landscape-vineyard-and-grapes-bunches-172588810.html.

15. Lanz, Evgenija. "Delicious german pretzels with butter." Depositphotos, depositphotos.com/photo/delicious-german-pretzels-with -butter-48097527.html.

16. M, M. "Hot mulled wine with oranges, anise and cinnamon." Depositphotos, depositphotos.com/vector/hot-mulled-wine-with-oranges -anise-and-cinnamon-86253878.html.

17. Maulana, Bahtiar. "Winter mountain landscape with fir trees." Depositphotos, depositphotos.com/vector/winter-mountain-landscape-wi th-fir-trees-173435404.html.

18. Miller, Olga. "Vector illustration of a deer family in the woods." Depositphotos, depositphotos.com/vector/vector-illustration-deer-family- woods-717214854.html.

19. Potysiev, Denis. "Pretzel. Vintage vector flat illustration." Depositphotos, depositphotos.com/vector/pretzel-vintage-vector-flat-illus tration-120157392.html.

20. Raths, Alexander. "Mulled wine on german christkindl

markt." Depositphotos,

depositphotos.com/photo/mulled-wine-on-german-christ

kindl-markt-56920965.html.

21. Rehak, Matyas. "Path at Triberg Waterfalls in the Black

Forest region in , Baden-Wuerttemberg, Germany."

Depositphotos,

depositphotos.com/photo/path-triberg-waterfalls-black-f

orest-region-baden-wuerttemberg-germany-661314702.h

tml.

22. Schwerin, Heinz-Peter. "Mummelsee in the Black Forest

Germany." Depositphotos,

depositphotos.com/photo/mummelsee-black-forest-ger

many-215832416.html.

23. Sereda, Tomas. "Underground train in mine, carts in gold,

silver and copper mine." Depositphotos,

depositphotos.com/photo/underground-train-in-mine-car

ts-in-gold-silver-and-copper-mine-18281683.html.

24. Steves, Rick. "Discovering the Romance of Germany's Black

Forest." Rick Steves, 16 Apr. 2024,

www.ricksteves.com/watch-read-listen/read/articles/blac

k-forest-germany-discovering-romance.

25. Zerndl, Andreas. "People Hiking at Feldberg Mountain in Spring." Depositphotos, depositphotos.com/photo/people-hiking-at-feldberg-mountain-in-spring-74008233.html.

Made in the USA
Las Vegas, NV
10 September 2024

95057227R00105